W9-ABE-564

J. R. MASTERMAN I. M. C.

BOOKS BY ZILPHA KEATLEY SNYDER

Black and Blue Magic
The Changeling
The Egypt Game
Eyes in the Fishbowl
The Headless Cupid
Season of Ponies
The Truth About Stone Hollow
The Velvet Room
The Witches of Worm
Below the Root
And All Between
Until the Celebration
The Famous Stanley Kidnapping Case
A Fabulous Creature
Come On, Patsy
The Birds of Summer

THE BIRDS OF SUMMER

MASTERMAN I M C

Zilpha Keatley Snyder

THE BIRDS
OF SUMMER

Atheneum **1 9 8 4**

NEW YORK

22568

LIBRARY OF CONGRESS CATALOGING IN PUBLICATION DATA
Snyder, Zilpha Keatley.
   The birds of summer.
   SUMMARY: Fifteen-year-old Summer, daughter of a
northern California flower child, is torn by confused
feelings and difficult relationships with friends,
employers and especially her mother.
   [1. California—Fiction. 2. Mothers and daughters—
Fiction] I. Title.
PZ7.S68522Bi 1983   [Fic]   82–13756
ISBN 0–689–30967–8
Copyright © 1983 by Zilpha Keatley Snyder
All rights reserved
Published simultaneously in Canada by
McClelland & Stewart, Ltd.
Composition by American–Stratford Graphic Services, Inc.
Brattleboro, Vermont
Printed and bound by Fairfield Graphics
Fairfield, Pennsylvania
Designed by Felicia Bond
First Printing January 1983
Second Printing February 1984

To Alla, Diane, Eileen,

Margaret, Mildred, Pat and Ruth

for advice, assistance and moral support;

and to two very special Elisabeths.

1

The test didn't take long. The Vonnegut story was an old favorite, so after a quick skim she was ready for the typically Pardellian questions about characterization and motivation. Pardell always asked about characterization and motivation. When she had finished, Summer folded the test and put it on the corner of the desk for the monitor and took out the letter she'd started the night before right after she'd found out about Oriole's latest fiasco. She didn't often write to Grant in class, especially not Pardell's class, but at that moment everyone was too busy with the test to notice, and the memory of what she'd written the night before was like a dark shadow crawling around the edges of her mind. After she'd read it over, she scratched out most of it.

I crossed out that last part because it wasn't entirely fair and rational—well, not rational, anyway. The thing is, I was really furious at Oriole when I wrote it. God knows why. I certainly ought to be used to

3

it by now. But this time she'd kept the job for three weeks and it actually seemed like there might be a chance. Not a very good one, maybe, but a lot better than usual, because baking bread is one thing Oriole really does well. Maybe you remember— she says you used to like her bread. And her boss at the Franklin House was very enthusiastic at first. All the customers were raving about it, especially the sourdough dill, which is her most recent specialty. And then she has to go and show up at work stoned out of her mind. So what else is new?

An itchy feeling that somebody was watching made Summer look up quickly to find Nicky Fisher staring at her. The stare, like everything about Nicky, was super high intensity—no wonder she felt it. She covered the letter with one hand and returned his stare, questioningly. He looked at the finished test on the edge of her desk and then, pointedly, at his watch. Then he grinned and shook his head in a way that said something like, "how do you do it?" or perhaps, "Summer McIntyre is a brain." She wrinkled her nose at him. Nicky was into paying compliments lately. In the last month or so he'd mentioned her brains at least half a dozen times—her hair nearly as many—her eyes once or twice—and once he'd even said he liked the way she dressed, which was really ridiculous and a good indication of just what a phony sexist hypocrite he was turning out to be. She knew enough about men—not that Nicky was one, although he obviously thought he was—to know why he'd switched to compliments instead of pulling her hair and kicking her in the shins the way he used to. She knew what he was up to when he stared at the front of her sweater and told her she had beautiful eyes. On the whole she preferred having her shins kicked. But for old times' sake—for all the years of being favorite enemies, for all the trees climbed and club houses built and violent arguments over who got to be Darth Vader or the Sundance Kid—she gave him a semi-friendly smile before going back to her letter. It took her a while to get back into the calm philosophical mood she always tried for in her letters to Grant.

Would you have been angry if you'd been there last night? At her for getting stoned and losing another job? Or maybe at me for yelling at her? Both probably. Except, if you'd been there perhaps none of it would have happened. It's something I think about sometimes—what it would have been like if you'd stayed and maybe even married Oriole. Not that I care about the marriage part. I really rather like being illegitimate. According to Pardell, bastards have been a significant sub-group, historically speaking. But sometimes I just wonder if you and Oriole would have gone sort of semi-establishment the way the Fishers did after they'd had three kids and inherited

5

the property. Oriole says you would have married her if you'd known about the pregnancy, but she says she's glad you didn't because this way you left her with only perfect things—the poems and the memories and me—and if you'd stayed the not so perfect things would have started the way they always do. Sometimes she says, "Grant left me the memory of one perfect summer and the beginning of another." Only she doesn't say that when she's mad at me like she was last night for yelling at her and telling her what a lousy mother she is. She didn't yell back though. She just got something she'd hidden in the flour sifter and went outside. I didn't exactly see what it was, but it was probably a joint. She was gone for a long time and I went around kicking things and yelling at Sparrow and Cerbe. Cerbe whimpered and Sparrow cried herself to sleep. Sparrow always cries when Oriole and I fight. I never cry anymore— but I didn't sleep much, either.

"Okay. That's it. Time's up. Fold your papers and put them on the corner of your desks where the trustees can find them, and you're all at large, God help us, until tomorrow morning."

Alan J. Pardell, who had taught Sophomore English at Alvarro High for a long time, was a tall man with a face and head like an aging chewed-up lion. He blamed what he called his "desultory nose"

6

on an early career as a sparring partner for several famous boxers, but nobody knew if that was the truth or just part of the Pardell mythology. The "Warden Pardell" bit was a favorite part of the myth so everyone grinned, even the ones who were still writing frantically. Nearly everyone laughed at Pardell's jokes, even now in April after months of funnies about the terror-stricken warden in charge of a bunch of teen-age public enemies. It was hard to say why they went on laughing, except it made it funnier when Pardell carried on about "doing time" in Sophomore English because it was the one class that never felt like a jail term. And when he pretended to hate and fear his students, what made people laugh was knowing, without his ever saying, how he really felt. So when he took the roll and gasped, "My God! You're all here. It's a plot, isn't it? There's going to be a riot?" everyone cracked up, even the radical types who usually made it a point never to laugh at any teacher's jokes.

Summer was halfway down the hall when Nicky caught up with her. "Hey, slow down," he said. "I've got some dynamite stuff. Want to meet me in the parking lot?" and then taking in her frown, without even a pause for breath, "Well, how about a root beer at the Pelican?" She shook her head. "Some ice cream? A double dip? Butterscotch and fudge ripple?" It was tempting, especially the fudge ripple, but she went on shaking her head

"I can't," she said finally. "Sparrow's waiting for me." She grinned. "You want to buy her one, too?"

Nicky made a face. "Not really. What's with this big-sister bit all of a sudden?"

"It's not all of a sudden. I've been walking home with Sparrow ever since Marina went away. It's too far for her to walk all alone."

Nicky's gaze, fixed as usual on the front of her blouse, flickered and shifted. Summer watched him, wondering about the shifty eyes and why he didn't say any of the things you might expect under the circumstances. Things like, "Yeah, it's too bad about Marina," or, "Marina misses her, too." She'd noticed it before—how any mention of his little sister, who'd been sent to live with relatives because of her asthma, seemed to make him uneasy. But this time his behavior struck her as really peculiar—almost strange enough to make her wonder if Sparrow's latest fantasy about Marina was so ridiculous after all.

It was only natural that Sparrow was upset about Marina. Growing up on the hill with no other kids their age around, they were as close as sisters, or closer. So when Sparrow started pretending—playing with an imaginary Marina—Summer hadn't been very surprised. Lots of kids have imaginary companions. But what had happened on Saturday was different. On Saturday it became clear that Sparrow really believed that Marina had come home, or else had never actually gone away at all.

"About Marina and Sparrow—" Summer began, but Nicky interrupted.

"Hey, there's Judson with his new wheels. See you tomorrow," and he hurried off to where Dan Judson was just pulling up in front of the school

8

with a car load of other guys—flakes mostly, whose vocabularies, when stretched to their outside limits, just barely covered cars, beer and girls, in that order. Halfway down the slope Nicky looked back and waved and hurried on. There was a definite feeling that he was glad to get away, and for some reason, it made her a little bit angry. Not that she cared about Nicky Fisher deserting her for a bunch of flakes. It was just another example of what a hypocrite he was turning out to be. If he didn't want to talk about Sparrow and Marina, why didn't he just say so? She shrugged her shoulders and headed east across town toward the elementary school.

In spite of the fact that most of the town lay between the two schools, the walk didn't take very long. Although its full name was Alvarro Bay City, the "city" part was an obvious euphemism—village would be more like it. A village in size as well as in picturesque charm . . . and also in the way its inhabitants lived in their own little world in which everyone knew a great deal about everyone else and people moved in tightly spun circles that overlapped only in certain special ways.

Sometimes Summer thought that she was probably the only person in the world who had any doubts about the perfection of Alvarro Bay City. Tourists raved about its setting, high on the headlands overlooking the Pacific Ocean, and the quaint charm of its buildings, many of which reflected the New England origins of the earliest settlers.

She'd give it quaintness and charm, all right—and fog-softened air and vacant-lot jungles full of wild nasturtiums and surrounding hillsides where redwood groves formed towering green cathedrals—and still count the days until she could get the hell out of Alvarro Bay City and out of any town where everybody knew, or thought they knew, everything about everybody else.

It was 3 :45 by the time she reached the elementary school and most of the kids had gone home long before. Except for four or five little boys playing kickball way out on the diamond, there was no one in sight except Sparrow. All alone in the playground area, she was hanging upside down, her long braids almost touching the ground and her face almost as red as her hair. When she saw Summer, she yelled and waved and went on hanging.

"Your face is really red," Summer said. "You'd better stop that before you have a hemorrhage or something."

"Five hundred and seventy-six, five hundred and seventy-seven," Sparrow said.

"Sparrow. I mean it. You nose is going to start bleeding again." Summer moved purposefully forward, but Sparrow waved her away frantically and went on counting. "Five hundred and eighty-two," she screamed despairingly as Summer grabbed her around the thighs and pulled her off the bar.

"You ruined it. You ruined my new record. I was just about to beat Marina's record." Sitting on the ground, Sparrow frowned fiercely and rubbed the backs of her knees, while her bright red face slowly faded to its usual pale tan, sprinkled with tiny golden freckles.

10

It occurred to Summer to wonder if the record in question was established some weeks ago by the flesh and blood Marina, or more recently by a fantasy version—but she didn't ask. At the moment she was feeling too hungry and tired to cope with imaginary acquaintances—real ones were bad enough—but she might as well have asked. Sparrow volunteered the information immediately—and continuously—all the way home. Just as Summer had suspected, the record was a new one supposedly established since Marina's return. "She is home again," Sparrow kept saying. "I know she is, Summer. Last night she looked in the window and told me she was home again and I should come up right away to see her."

"Look," Summer said finally, "I'm not trying to get on your case about lying, or anything. I used to have . . ." She stopped. She had never told anyone about the Grant thing and she didn't intend to start now. ". . . an invisible friend, too," she went on. "But if you want me to help you, you have to tell me the truth. The absolutely real no-pretending truth. You know what I mean. Seven years is plenty old enough to know what's absolutely real and what isn't. Have you really seen Marina lately?"

"Look out," Sparrow yelled suddenly. "Here comes another one." They were walking along the shoulder of the highway, and as the car came by heading north she jumped as high as she could into the air. It was a game called Jumping Shadows that Summer had started years ago, before it began to bother her to be stared at by the startled people in the passing cars. "You didn't jump," Sparrow said. "You got shadowed. You're poisoned."

"Stop it! I asked you a question. Are you going to answer it or what?"

Sparrow looked uncomfortable. "I don't know. I mean, I don't know for sure about seeing Marina. I thought it was for sure. But then all of a sudden she wasn't there anymore, at the window, and I didn't see her go away or anything. She looked in the window and said for me to come to her house right away, and then she wasn't there anymore, and you said to lie down and quit pulling the covers off."

"You were dreaming," Summer said.

"Dreaming?" Sparrow's rounded forehead puckered into a frown. She looked puzzled, bewildered, but then suddenly she jutted her chin and said, "But the troll wasn't a dream. The troll was real and no-pretending."

"Yeah," Summer said. "You told me." It seemed that Marina had a secret place inside a rotted-out tree stump halfway up the hill, and on Saturday Sparrow had sneaked off and gone there. Summer was away working at Crown Ridge Ranch at the time—Sparrow never tried to sneak off when Summer was around—and Oriole hadn't even noticed that Sparrow had been gone, until she came back all excited about finding Marina's troll doll.

"You sure it wasn't there all along? I mean ever since she left?"

"No. No," Sparrow shouted. "It wasn't. I've been there before, and it wasn't there. But then it was there, all of a sudden, right on a little shelf place where she always used to put it. Marina came to our secret place and put it there, not long ago. I know she did."

"Couldn't someone else have done it? Lots of people have those little troll dolls."

"No! No! It was Marina's troll. She braided its hair and drew it a moustache with a ball point. Its name was Adam."

Summer smiled. Adam was Marina's oldest and not favorite brother. Like Jerry, his father, Adam was dark and solemn and into telling everyone else how they should run their lives. He was also very ambitious and hardworking, which got him a lot of strokes from adult types. Nicky, who was two years younger, seemed to admire and hate Adam a lot, and Marina always said he was bossy. Undoubtedly she'd named the ugly doll after him to tease him. "Okay," Summer said. "So the troll doll was Adam. There are still other ways it could have gotten on that shelf."

"What other ways?"

Another car came by just then and Sparrow stopped to get ready to jump, and by the time she caught up with Summer she'd forgotten what she'd asked, which was just as well, since Summer really didn't have an answer in mind. It didn't seem likely that either Adam or Nicky, who were seventeen and fifteen, had been playing with dolls. And no other kids lived anywhere near the Fishers' property.

The gravel road led up through the Fishers' property, first passing the pathway to the McIntyres' trailer and then fishtailing on up the mountain to the high plateau on which Jerry and Galya had built their new house and planted their organic gardens. By the time they turned off the highway onto the Fishers' road, Summer was walking fast—tuning out Sparrow's continuing chatter. An ominous tightness in her stomach was threatening to become something more unless, by hurrying, she managed to get home first. In the large grove of redwoods where she often stopped for a moment to breathe in the everlasting calm of the great trees, she only pushed on faster, until Sparrow had to trot to keep beside her. Beyond the redwoods the road became a narrow canyon, enclosed now by dense stands of fir and pine and an impenetrable undergrowth of madrone and wild rhododendron. Summer was jogging now, and in less than ten minutes they reached the beginning of the footpath. As she turned onto the path, Sparrow grabbed her hand and pulled her to a stop.

"Let's go on up to the Fishers'," she said. "I want to ask Galya if Marina is back. Come with me, Summer. Please."

Summer jerked her hand away. "No. You know we can't do that. You know what Jerry told us about not going up there because of the new dog. He said we shouldn't ever go up there anymore unless they know we're coming, so they can tie up the dog."

"I'm not afraid of that dog."

"Well, you ought to be. Jerry said it's very dangerous. So you stay away from there. Do you hear me?" Summer felt angry—tense with the antsy feeling she always got when she was almost home—a feeling that lasted until she found Oriole and saw how she was and what she was doing.

14

"Well, then. Let's tell them we're coming," Sparrow said brightly, as if it were the simplest thing in the world.

"How are we going to do that?" Oriole, quoting Esau, her old hippie guru, was always saying that going without a telephone was freeing yourself from the strangling umbilical cord of the establishment. But at the moment, a bit of establishment umbilical cord would certainly solve Sparrow's problem.

"Look," she told Sparrow. "Why don't you sit here by the road and watch for Jerry's truck. If you see him, you can tell him we want to visit and ask him to shut up the dog. Okay? But don't you go up there by yourself. Promise?"

After Sparrow had promised and double-promised and seated herself on a stump, Summer started down the path that led to the trailer—"The McIntyre Trailer" as it was called, because Oriole McIntyre and her daughters had lived there for more than seven years, but it actually belonged to the Fishers, as did the land it sat on. Nicky had been born there in the tiny room that Summer shared with Sparrow, and he had always enjoyed telling Summer that she was sleeping in his bedroom. None of the teasing techniques in Nicky's long and obnoxious repertoire made her angrier, and someday she was going to tell him exactly what he could do with his room and his trailer and every inch of the land it sat on.

In days of luxurious double-wides set in landscaped parks, the Fisher/McIntyre mobile home was definitely an anachronism. Galya and Jerry had hauled it to its present resting place, in a small clear-

15

ing surrounded by dense forest, more than fifteen years before when the land still belonged to Galya's old Russian grandfather. It hadn't been until several years later, when Galya's Dyedushka had died leaving her all his property, that she and Jerry had gotten married, built a huge new log house near Dyedushka's old one, and started their organic farming business. The trailer had been deserted for a while and then loaned or rented to various lame duck projects of Galya's, before Oriole and company arrived on the scene. Oriole and Summer and Danny it had been then, and the beginnings of Sparrow, although that hadn't become evident until sometime later.

Summer had been only seven years old at the time, but she could remember the day they moved in clearly, and how pleased she'd been with the trailer. It must have been pretty decrepit even then, but she'd liked the flickering propane lights and tiny bathroom, and it must have seemed luxurious compared to some of the places they'd been living. She had clear memories of that first day and then nothing much until an afternoon several months later when Sparrow was born. Summer had sat on the steps listening and crying while Galya, who'd had some training as a midwife, helped Oriole give birth. Danny had still been there that day, because Summer remembered his coming out to talk to her on the steps, but he'd disappeared soon afterwards, as all of Oriole's men seemed to do sooner or later. But by then Galya and Oriole had become very tight, and even more important, Galya's baby Marina and Sparrow had become even tighter. So the Fishers went on letting Oriole live in the trailer, even when she didn't pay the rent for months at a time. Oriole was always saying they were going to move, but they never did and probably never would, unless the Fishers threw them out. Or, unless Summer did something about it, which she definitely planned to do just as soon as she possibly could.

It was on the last turn of the trail, when the trailer suddenly came into view, that the uneasy tension in her stomach knotted into an ache, and something she'd been squeezing back into the far edges of her mind escaped in an overpowering flood. Careless of the rough surface of the path, she began to run at top speed, stumbling and nearly falling, her heart thudding against her ribs. She had reached the steps when Cerbe shot out of the bushes and raced her up the stairs, almost knocking her off her feet. Pushing him violently aside, she threw the door open—and stopped.

Oriole was standing by the sink peeling carrots. Her wild red hair was combed and tied back with a ribbon, and she was wearing the pleated blue skirt that Summer had bought for her at a church rummage sale—which she hardly ever wore.

"Hi, baby." Oriole's voice, always breathy and tremulous, was no more so than usual.

Summer closed the door carefully and slowly while she stilled her face and blanked her eyes. Then, as if bringing herself back with difficulty from an absorbing daydream, she turned back to face her mother. "Oh hi," she said.

2

In the bedroom Summer put her books away, sat down on the edge of the bed and waited for the pain in her stomach to fade and for the ridiculous tremors to stop running up and down the backs of her legs. Clenching her fists until her nails pinched her palms and biting her lower lip, she punished her body for its crazy reactions. She had always blamed her body because her mind, at least the conscious and reasonable part of it, knew how stupid it was to get into such a state over nothing. Even years ago, when the sudden senseless attacks of anxiety had been almost a daily thing, she had never been certain just what it was she was afraid might have happened. In those days she had never even tried to figure it out—as if knowing what it might be could somehow make it come true. So she could only run home, shaking and panting like some kind of psycho, until she found Oriole and saw that everything was all right.

But for the same thing to happen now, when she was almost sixteen years old and able to reason—now

18

when she was able to imagine the worst and know that it wouldn't be the end of the world—for the same kind of mindless panic to return now was just too frustrating. In the last few weeks she'd almost begun to hope that she'd outgrown it. But it had always been worse when something had gone particularly wrong —like last night.

At first when Cerbe tried to nuzzle her hands away from her face, she shoved him back angrily; but then, when he whined mournfully, she peeked out from between her fingers.

Cerbe was a big mutt, probably half german shepherd and half husky. He had been named Cerbe, Cerberus really, after another dog—one Grant had adopted during the summer he'd lived with Oriole. That Cerberus had died when Summer was still a baby, but she'd heard a lot about him from Oriole's "good-old-days" stories. So, when Cerbe had appeared on the scene, a half-grown pup that someone had dumped beside the road, he'd become Cerberus the second and had grown into a wooly bear of a dog, shaggy, smelly, and at the moment, dramatically woebegone. Cerbe had always been a ham.

Because his drooping tail and head and sad doggy eyebrows were just too much, she grabbed him roughly and pulled him against her chest, her fingers deep in the thick fur on each side of his broad body. With the top of his shaggy bear-shaped head pushing against her stomach, he nuzzled happily, crooning his love growl, and she growled back. Her face buried in his rough coat, she whispered insults about his looks and intelligence and the doggy funkiness of his smell

19

—loving him fiercely for knowing how she felt about him no matter what she said or did. A few minutes later she went out, steady-handed, to talk to Oriole.

"Here. Have a carrot?" Oriole said. Not only had she combed her hair and dressed in her straightest clothes, but she was actually wearing shoes. Obviously she was sorry about what happened last night and was trying to make amends. That was Oriole for you—thinking a hair ribbon could solve the McIntyres' problems. Talk about straightening the deck chairs on the *Titanic!*

Summer accepted the vegetable peace offering and sat down at the table. Leaning on her elbows she crunched on the carrot and watched Oriole speculatively, waiting for the next gesture. The kitchen area was cleaner than usual. Most of the dishes were done except for the ones on the window ledge that had been there for so long they'd become semi-permanent, like a part of the decor. The cracked and chipped surface of the Formica sinkboard had been wiped, and it looked as if dinner was already underway. Putting a dish of raw vegetables on the table, Oriole sat down facing Summer.

"The pay was terrible, anyway," she said. "When I realized what it would do to our food stamp allowance—"

"Mother!" She never called Oriole that except when she was really furious at her. "That's not true, and you know it. We figured it all out, remember? Even with the reduction in the AFDC, we'd have been getting almost two hundred more . . ." She stopped suddenly and shrugged. The job was over—

20

gone—lost forever, so it didn't make any difference.

"Galya stopped by this morning and took me in to see about the food stamps. We're not going to have to wait to be reinstated. That's good news, isn't it?"

"Great!" She could almost taste the bitterness in her voice. Oriole looked at her sharply.

"I don't see why you're so uptight about food stamps. Esau used to say that we should never be ashamed of having food stamps. Esau said food should be free to everyone, like air and sunshine, and it's a crime that some people should have more than others just because they have more money. Esau always said, 'Just smile sweetly right into the faces of people who glare at you in the checkout line because—'"

"Yeah, I know," Summer interrupted. "I remember what Esau always said."

"Do you really remember him? You were only about four when the Tribe broke up."

"No. I don't remember him. It's hearing you tell about him that I remember." Esau had been the leader and guru of a group of people that Oriole had lived with for a while in San Francisco. The Angel Tribe, as they'd called themselves, had inhabited a big old house only a few blocks from the center of Haight-Ashbury, right in the midst of everything that was going on in those days. And Oriole had been right in the center of the Angel Tribe; she still loved to remember and talk about it. Summer had heard over and over again about how the big old house had been painted purple with orange shutters and the windows draped with tie-dyed sheets, and how the people

21

going by used to stop and stare. And how she, Oriole, had been Esau's special old lady for a while and a real celebrity in the Haight, and even in the whole city, because some reporter on the *Berkeley Barb* had chosen her to do a picture story on—as the ultimate flower child. "A beautiful barefoot nymph in a cloud of red-gold hair, with a lovely, dark-eyed hippie baby astride her hip." Summer had heard that particular phrase so many times she could quote it by heart, and she could recognize her own dark eyes and level brows in the baby's round face. But she really couldn't remember the Angel Tribe, or even Esau. What she did remember, and probably could never forget as long as she lived, was hearing Oriole tell about all of it over and over again, while she carefully unfolded the yellowing clipping from the *Berkeley Barb*.

"It's really too bad you can't remember Esau," Oriole said. "He was so crazy about you. He was always saying what a wonderful human being you were going to turn out to be because of being raised in such a free and loving environment."

"Yeah. I know. Too bad he wasn't right."

Oriole, who had been deciding betwen a carrot or a celery stick, looked up quickly, her smile uncertain —obviously wondering if Summer's remark was repentant, or simply sarcastic. Actually, it was both. She was ashamed of the way she had treated Oriole the night before, but at the same time she was bitter about a lot of things, among which was the "free and loving" environment in which she had been raised. Free and loving could mean a lot of things, and some of them she could have done without. But her answering smile was only a little grudging, and Oriole's immediately broadened into happy relief.

"So," she said, "how was school today? Did the test go all right?" And Summer began to tell her about the test, and a discussion she'd had with Haley, and about watching Nicky trying to impress Kid Christopher. It wasn't until almost an hour later that she remembered about Sparrow. She'd been imitating Kid approaching a bunch of girls, like a banty rooster dragging his wings through a flock of hens, when she suddenly remembered—and stopped in mid-strut.

"Hey. Where's Sparrow?" she said.

It took Oriole a while to stop laughing. Whenever Oriole laughed it took her a while to stop. "Why?" she said finally. "Didn't she come home with you?"

"She was waiting out by the road for some of the Fishers to go by so she could ask them to shut up the dog. She wants to go up there."

Oriole's smile was rueful. "I'm afraid she's wasting her time. I mean, even if she gets to talk to Jerry, he probably won't let her visit. Galya says he's on some kind of a bummer lately, and it would be best if none of us go up there for a while."

Already on her way to get her sweater, Summer looked back, and just as she suspected, Oriole's smile was only partly concealing something uncomfortable. Hurt, maybe, because Galya, her oldest and best friend, didn't want her hanging around—or anxiety because so much depended on keeping the Fishers' good will. A wave of resentment made Summer's face burn: a sweeping kind of resentment that covered a lot of things but finally focused on Oriole for her

23

cringing smile and for sitting there being pathetic while Sparrow was God-knows-where. She grabbed her sweater, ran out the door and let it bang after her. A moment later it slammed again as Cerbe charged after her.

Just as she had feared, Sparrow was no longer sitting beside the road. Summer called loudly and angrily three or four times and then began to run. She had been running at top speed for several minutes when she rounded a turn and caught up with Sparrow, trudging along beside the road. When she saw Summer, Sparrow's big eyes widened and her jaw dropped.

"Don't be mad, Summer," she said. "I wasn't going to go all the way. I was just going to go as far as Marina's tree house. That dog won't see me if I just go that far."

Summer had just grabbed Sparrow by the arm and was about to start yelling at her when the roar of a car motor seemed to be all around them. There was barely time to scramble to the side of the road before Jerry Fisher's green pickup tore around the corner and, a few yards beyond them, skidded to a stop. But the man who got out of the cab was not Jerry.

Tall and narrow, with a sleek, dark face like an old-fashioned ad for hair tonic, the man who climbed out of the pickup and slowly and deliberately sauntered across the road, was a complete stranger. "Well, well," he said. "What have we here?" He was smiling, but the smile, outlined by a thin black moustache, was somehow anything but reassuring. When he was very close, so close she could smell him—sweat and a

24

musty aftershave lotion—he stopped, folded his arms across his chest and stared, still smiling the threatening smile. For a moment no one said or did anything, but then Sparrow made a whimpering noise and immediately a growl began to rumble in Cerbe's throat. The smile disappeared from the man's face.

"Hey, Bart!" he yelled. "Come here."

The second man was enormous, with a huge head of bushy hair and a red, heavy-jawed face. As he got out of the truck, he reached into the back and got out a heavy club-shaped tree branch. Panic surged in Summer's throat, and grabbing Cerbe's collar and Sparrow's arm, she began to back away down the road. Grinning again, the two men just stood there, watching them go. But when they were several yards away, the bushy-haired man suddenly hunched his shoulders, raised his club and rushed at them, making a noise like a roaring lion. Sparrow screamed and fled down the road. Cerbe went crazy, growling fiercely and standing on his hind legs in his eagerness to attack. It was all Summer could do to hang onto his collar and drag him with her as she continued to back away. Then the thin man laughed and sauntered back to the truck. After a moment the big Neanderthal-type followed, swinging his club jauntily. Still hanging on to Cerbe's collar, Summer ran for home— fuming with outraged anger.

"Oh, they're probably just some of the Fishers' friends," was all Oriole said when Summer told her what had happened. "Or Jude's. That's probably it. They're probably friends of Jude from San Francisco." Jude was a scrawny burned-out type of indefi-

25

nite age who'd been hanging around Alvarro Bay off and on for a long time. Once, years before, Galya had rescued him from a ditch somewhere and nursed him back to health on organic vegetables and clean country air. Eventually he'd drifted back to the city and to the hard stuff, but almost every spring he cleaned up his act enough to turn up at the Fishers' for a summer of work in the vegetable gardens and comparatively clean living.

"But why would they be driving Jerry's truck?" Summer said. "You know how uptight he is about it. Adam isn't allowed to drive it unless Jerry's with him, and Nicky says he isn't even allowed to look at it."

Oriole shrugged. "Well, why don't you just ask Nicky about them? He must know who they are."

It was Summer's turn to shrug. Maybe she'd ask Nicky and maybe she wouldn't. Since he'd started reacting to the simplest "hi" as if it were some kind of sexual provocation, she'd made it a rule not to initiate even the most casual conversation with him. But, on the other hand, she was very curious about the two strangers—curious and uneasy, not to mention angry. It still made her furious when she thought about the way the big hulking one had rushed at them. She hated even to think about what might have happened if she hadn't been able to hang onto Cerbe's collar. The incident kept reappearing in her mind all evening, and at last she decided she would ask Nicky— if the opportunity arose.

As it happened, the opportunity did arise, the next afternoon while she was talking to Haley on the front steps of the school. Haley Skinner was, or at least had

26

been, one of Summer's best friends. All through elementary school Haley and Summer had been very tight, and during that time the Skinners—Haley and her parents and her two older sisters—had been like a second family to Summer. In fact, some people might have said they were her only family, traditionally speaking. Mr. John Skinner, who was a banker, liked people and money; and his wife, Adele, loved antiques and cooking and gossip. For a while, when she was quite young, Summer had considered them an ideal family.

During those years Summer and Haley had started a Buckminster Fuller fan club together, entered joint projects in two science fairs and coauthored the first seventy-two pages of a novel that was going to be the *Peyton Place* of Alvarro Bay City. They also got the best grades in most of their classes, usually Summer first and Haley second, although it could easily have been the other way around if Haley had been willing to work at it. But even then Haley Skinner never worked hard at anything except having fun. But in junior high the Summer-Haley thing had begun to fall apart, and lately they only met now and then to argue—as they were doing on the steps. Haley was trying to get Summer to say she would come to a beach party.

"It'll be freezing cold," Summer said.

"Who cares," Haley said, her eyebrows twitching the way they always did when she talked about sex. "There'll be plenty of blankets. Kid even offered to bring his car blanket."

"Great," Summer said. "Will he wash it first?"

27

Kid Christopher had the reputation of being a world-class devirginizer, and according to local legend, his car blanket had figured in a great many of his exploits. "The Blanket" was a favorite topic of conversation among his friends and admirers and would-be imitators like Nicky Fisher. Once someone had lifted it and hung it up on the gym door with girls' names on paper arrows pinned all over it.

"Wash it?" Haley said. "Don't be ridiculous."

It was just about then that Nicky came out the door, took one look at them and kept on going. Nicky would never have admitted it, but the truth was that Haley, with her quick, sharp-edged wit, had always intimidated him. Still pretending not to have noticed them, he was starting down the stairs when Haley yelled, "Hey, Fisher. Come over here."

"Hey," Nicky said, acting surprised. His swagger as he walked over, the way he leaned against the wall and just looked for a moment before he said anything and the way he raised his eyebrows as he said, "*Ciao,*" were all obvious imitations of Kid—only when Kid did them, they worked.

"Well!" Haley said, grinning sarcastically. "Chow-chow-chow to you, too, lover boy."

Nicky laughed too loudly, took his hand down off the wall and couldn't think of any place to put it. To cover his confusion, Summer found herself saying, "Haley wants to ask if you're going to the beach party."

"Oh yeah?" Nicky said. "Sure, I'm going."

"Way to go, Fisher," Haley said. "Now see if you can talk this hung-up unit into showing up. She says

28

she can't make it." She waved and started down the steps. "I got to go meet someone," she called. "Go for it, Fisher."

As soon as Haley was out of sight, Nicky was his old self again. "You going?" he asked enthusiastically, his eyes busy, as usual.

"No," she said flatly. "Look, Nicky. I want to ask you about something. Yesterday two weird guys in your father's truck almost ran over Sparrow and me. And then they stopped and got out and acted really strange. One of them had a big club and I thought for a minute that he was going to hit Cerbe with it. Who are they, anyway?"

"Two guys?" Nicky looked startled, stunned almost. "Oh yeah. Yeah, they're—they're friends of Jude's. Yeah. Jude met them in San Francisco." Even though he never quit trying, Nicky had never been able to fool her, and he wasn't fooling her at that moment. It was clear that something about her question really bothered him, and he was undoubtedly lying to her.

"How come they were driving your dad's truck?"

"Oh that. My dad probably sent them for something. They're working for us—helping out with the vegetables."

"Oh yeah?" Summer let her surprise show. She remembered hearing Galya say that there actually wasn't enough work or money to justify hiring Jude, except that he was willing to work for very little because he liked the country and Galya's cooking. "Are you planting more than usual?"

Nicky stared for a moment before he answered.

29

3

She said she'd never met him before and he just happened to come by as she was on her way to mail a letter. So—when he offered her a ride into town she remembered she needed to buy some wheat germ, or something, so she said yes. His name is Angelo, believe-it-or-not, and he told her he was helping the Fishers build some new greenhouses. I asked her if she'd happened to mention the way he and the Frankenstein's monster look-alike tried to scare Sparrow and me to death, and she said she did, and he explained that it was just a joke. A joke! Can you imagine? If Cerbe had gotten away from me, there wouldn't have been anything funny about it. I told her that both of them gave me the creeps, and she said I shouldn't be so negative and that, "Angelo seems like a very open and loving person." God! Where have I heard that before?

"Hey, look." Oriole's voice was loud and clear through the thin wood of the bedroom's sliding door. "I won."

"No, you didn't, you didn't win yet. You have to throw the exact amount. Summer says you have to throw the exact amount."

Oriole's laugh was like a little girl's, high-pitched and teasing. "No, you don't. Not the way I play. We're playing Oriole's rules today."

"Hey, you two," Summer shouted. "Hold it down. I can't concentrate."

" 'Scuse us!" Oriole shouted, and the voices became softer. Summer had locked herself in the bedroom to finish her homework, but the assignment hadn't taken long, and for the last half hour she'd been writing to Grant. Now with the voices in the next room reduced to a murmur, she returned to the letter.

> *I've been feeling strange lately—tense and jumpy. I don't know why exactly except that several things have happened that make me think that something weird is going on at the Fishers'. And now this Angelo character. I have a very strong feeling that this one is really bad news. I just wish . . .*

She sighed, wrote something, scratched it out and began to chew on the end of her pen. Her eyes wandered, coming to rest on the mirror on the opposite wall. The mirror was one of her most treasured possessions. It was very old and the glass was blotched and darkened, but the round frame had been covered

35

with peacock feathers. Carefully arranged to cover the cracked and blistered wood of the frame, the feathers curved out gracefully in a halo of shimmering color. In the old glass her own image was vaguely altered, transformed into someone intriguingly unfamiliar. A face from the past, perhaps, with mysterious, shadowy eyes and hollow cheeks ravaged by some great personal sorrow.

Behind her reflected face the blurs and cracks blended into shadowy vistas that, by squinting her eyes and using a little imagination, she could translate into a variety of interesting environments. To the left, a long blur could resemble a draped window and on the right a cluster of blotches might be interpreted as a stone fireplace. By adding a few extra details she could conjure up a complete room.

She had imagined the room before. It wouldn't be large but it would be perfect: the walls, the floor, the furniture—it would all be exactly right. She'd planned and replanned it a dozen times, using ideas garnered from magazines and store windows as well as, in several respects, Richard Oliver's study at Crown Ridge Ranch.

"Ha ha. I caught you. I caught you. You have to go back." Sparrow's noisy celebration, followed by Oriole's loud, "Shhhh!" and then the two of them giggling brought Summer back to reality. And reality was ten by ten, flimsy, leak-streaked and curled around the edges.

Once, a couple of years earlier, Summer had made an effort with the bedroom. She had painted the walls, built a long, narrow counter, which served as desk and dressing table, and padded two small nail kegs to use as stools. But Sparrow went right on throwing her things around, and Cerbe went on shedding all over the patch of carpet, and the rain came in again and streaked the newly painted walls. After that she pretty much gave up—except for the half of the counter that was strictly hers, which Sparrow avoided on pain of a mysteriously terrible fate, convincingly promised without ever being clearly defined. On that sacred ground, neatly arranged, there were always the same objects: a man's silver-backed hairbrush, several postcards under a sheet of window glass and a small wooden chest with a padlock.

The postcards were from Nan Oliver, mailed during trips to Europe and South America. The brush had been Grant's—the one thing he left behind, except for the poems and, of course, Summer herself. And the chest was full of letters.

Getting off the bed where she'd been sitting propped against the wall, she picked up the box and climbed back to the same spot, rearranging the pillows more comfortably behind her back. Because of a tight turtlenecked jersey, it took a moment to produce the key from where it always hung on a chain around her neck. When the padlock was unfastened, she returned the key to its hiding place before she opened the box. Taking the new letter from her binder, she added it to the ones already in the chest.

The letters, dozens and dozens of them, went back to the year she started second grade. They were written on every kind of paper: real stationery, binder paper, scraps of paper bag. Some of the early ones were even printed in straggly manuscript on the kind of wide-lined newsprint used by primary classes. When she added the new letter, she had to press down firmly in order to close the lid. She had no idea how many there were now. It had been a long time since she counted them. Suddenly she opened the box again, took out the entire stack, and turned it upside down. At the bottom of the box, along with her first bank book, was the first letter she'd ever written to Grant.

> *Dear Father,*
> *Today in school we are writing letters for Father's Day. Everyone is writing what good things their fathers do, like playing games and buying things. I think you would have too if you hadn't gone away to be a doctor. Mrs. Frasure says if I get an address she will mail my letter, but Oriole said you don't have one. Maybe I can get one for you.*
> *Love,*
> *Summer*

"What an idiot," Summer said. She pulled out several more of the oldest letters and looked through them. They were about school and playing with Haley and fighting with Nicky. A couple of times they mentioned the money she was saving to get an address for Grant. She couldn't remember what she thought an address was, but she must have thought it was something like an envelope.

As she leafed through the pile of letters, reading some and skimming others, she came across some that dealt with very private material—things she'd never told anyone else, not even Oriole. Or, in some cases, particularly not Oriole. There were, for instance, several mentions of Rif. Rif was a very handsome guy —a rock star, at least to hear him tell it—who had lived with them for a while after Danny left. Besides playing the guitar and singing, he made belts and wallets out of leather. He wasn't too bad most of the time, but when he was high he sometimes got nasty. Sparrow was still a baby then, and if she cried when he was trying to practice, it drove him up the wall. One of the leters, a long one, told about the time Rif had beaten Summer for kicking him in the shins. Oriole had been out somewhere, and Rif had started slapping Sparrow because she was crying, and it seemed like, this time, he wasn't going to stop. So Summer had kicked him hard. He'd beaten her with one of his handmade belts, and then he said that if she told anyone, he'd wring her neck. So she didn't tell, and Oriole didn't notice the bruises, so no one ever knew. Summer remembered that writing to Grant about the beating had made her feel better, even though she must have known by then about addresses and that Grant's was gone forever.

The truth about Grant's address was something she'd pieced together gradually over a period of years. Oriole's original statement—that "he didn't have one"—wasn't exactly the whole story. Sometime later she'd explained that Grant had left his parents' address in Chicago when he went away, and that for a time there had been an exchange of letters. But Oriole had stopped writing when she moved in with the Angel Tribe, and Grant had finally stopped, too.

Then someone had stolen the bag in which Oriole had been keeping his letters. By the time Summer began to ask about his address, Oriole had forgotten everything except for the city and that the street name was some kind of tree. Once Summer had mailed a letter to Grant Wilson, Tree Street, Chicago, but it had come back marked "insufficient address." But by then the letters had become a habit, so she'd gone on writing.

Many of the letters were about things like friends and teachers and books she happened to be reading. But as she got older they were also full of plans. Plans for college and medical school and, if everything went well, a career as a doctor. One particularly dealt with getting away from Alvarro Bay—to find out about other places and about herself—about who Summer would be if she weren't Summer McIntyre of Alvarro Bay. That reminded her of a poem, and she began to look for it.

She found it a little farther down, among letters written during the eighth grade. She'd had Mrs. Simpson, who was a poetry nut, for English that year, and a lot of the letters she wrote that year included poetry—like the one she'd remembered.

> *When I see Rome,*
> *And walk in ancient footprints,*
> *It won't be summer.*
>
> *It may be winter,*
> *When I tread the streets of long dead kings.*
> *Bridges of heroes, and the halls of fame.*

40

I'll flee through bright new spring
And withering fall,
Without a name.

But if you want me then,
Don't ever call
For summer

A great many of the letters mentioned the bank account—keeping Grant up to date on how it was progressing—if you call about fifty cents a week progress. In the days before she had a steady job, when she only picked up occasional baby-sitting and odd-job money, that was about par. It was only since Crown Ridge that the deposits had started to increase.

Among the more recent letters there were several about Crown Ridge Ranch and the Olivers. The first one, about a year and a half old now, told about the day Summer found the notice on the post office bulletin board. The letter started:

> *Guess what? I've got a real job. Last Friday I went in the post office to see if Oriole's check had come and I saw this woman in English riding clothes pinning a card on the bulletin board. As soon as she left, I read it, and it said that the Olivers at Crown Ridge Ranch were looking for someone to do housework one or two days a week. The minute I read the notice I decided I was going to try to get the job.*
>
> *I knew about the place. It's a ranch where they raise Arabians, but all you can*

see from the highway is pastures with white fences and lots of beautiful horses. Way back from the road among the trees you can get just a glimpse of a house and some barns.

So I went out there on Saturday morning. There was a number to call on the card, but I thought it would be better if I just went. The bus driver let me out right at the gate, but for quite a while I just sat on the fence trying to get up my nerve to walk up the driveway. The thing was, the notice said that they preferred a mature person and that references would be necessary. I'd taken along the letter Mrs. Slater had given me about the good job I did at the day care center, so I wasn't too worried about the reference thing, but I wasn't sure whether the Olivers would consider thirteen, almost fourteen really, mature enough. But from the minute I started up the driveway I quit being worried. I don't know why exactly, except I just knew I was going to get the job. And it wasn't just because I threw away the notice card, either. It was more that I knew I could do it better than anyone else because —well, because I really wanted to, I guess.

That particular letter ended there, but the next three or four were mostly about Crown Ridge Ranch and Richard and Nan Oliver. There was one almost entirely devoted to the house—the long low house sheltering from the ocean winds under a heavy shake roof—and another describing the barn with its enor-

42

mous hayloft and heated stalls. There was also quite a lot about the horses.

Before she'd started working at Crown Ridge, Summer had never even been close to a horse, and unlike a lot of kids she knew, she'd never particularly wanted to be. The way she felt was that anything that big ought to be more straightforward about its intentions. Like a dog, for instance, who lets you know right away how he's feeling about you. But she'd been immediately fascinated by the Crown Ridge Arabians, with their high arching necks and delicate faces. So fascinated, in fact, that she had gone to work early one morning so she would have time to sit on the fence and watch them for a while before Nan got up. She'd arrived early that first time simply because of the horses. What had happened had been entirely unplanned, but afterwards she'd gone on doing it for more reasons than one.

She'd been sitting there watching the young colts chase each other around the field like a bunch of overexcited first-graders, when she heard something and turned around to find Nan Oliver watching her. Then Nan climbed up on the fence beside her and started talking about how she'd done the same thing many times—sitting for hours and hours (which actually was a lot more than Summer had had in mind) just staring at horses like you'd look at a work of art in a museum. And, as they were climbing down to go indoors, Nan put her arm around Summer's shoulders and gave her a little hug. So after that she'd gone on arriving early to watch the horses—knowing that Nan Oliver was watching her.

But that was only Nan. Her husband, Mr. Richard Barrington Oliver, was a different matter. Summer had been working at Crown Ridge for several weekends before she even met him, because he was always away on business trips—and their first encounter turned out to be something of a disaster. She sifted through the stack until she found the letter she'd written about that first meeting.

> *Well, Mr. Richard Oliver came home today and I'm afraid I didn't make a very good impression. Not that there was anything I could have done about it. The thing is, Nan had been telling me that she couldn't promise me the job would be permanent, even though I'd been doing great, until her husband came home and approved of the arrangement. Either she read my mind or else she finally realized how totally unliberated that sounded, because she started explaining how she didn't have very good judgment about hiring people so she'd promised Richard she wouldn't do it anymore without consulting him. Anyway, she made it clear that making a good impression on old Richard B. was going to be pretty crucial, and I'd been plotting how I was going to come on beaucoup mature and efficient—and then he walks in while Nan is out in the barn and right into the bathroom where I'm practically standing on my head scrubbing the bathtub. I'd heard someone in the bedroom, but I thought it was Nan so*

I didn't pay any attention, and then suddenly there was this strange man walking through the bathroom unzipping his pants. I was startled at first and then, when I realized who it was, really twitchy, because my hair was hanging in my eyes and I'd made this ridiculous squeaky scream when I saw him. He was embarrassed, too, and then mad. And he was still mad a little later when I overheard him talking to Nan and telling her that she was incorrigible and he thought she'd advertised for a housekeeper, not a foster child.

The letter ended there, and the next one, written several days later, told about being called into Richard Oliver's study and told that, for the time being at least, she could keep the job. When she went in, he was sitting at his antique rolltop desk. He nodded and motioned for her to sit down, and went on writing. He wrote for a long time, and the longer she sat there, the more certain she became that she'd lost the job. So, when he finally said she hadn't, she was so relieved she didn't even feel angry at him for making her suffer so long for no reason. At least she hadn't been angry until later, when she'd had time to think about it.

Actually, the whole thing had been standard operating procedure for Richard Oliver. It hadn't taken Summer long to realize that the "making-people-wait" bit was just one of a whole repertoire of tricks that Oliver used to make people feel threatened and inferior—even people he had no real power over—so that when he was ready to deal with them they were so relieved they went right along with whatever he had in mind. Since that day she'd watched the way he related to quite a few other people and wondered if it was something he got from being so rich, or if it was how he'd gotten rich in the first place.

Learning how to deal with Richard Oliver hadn't been quite as easy as sitting on a fence staring at horses, but in the end the results were just about the same. Oliver never talked about her job being temporary anymore, and she'd even overheard him telling someone what a great find she'd been. She wasn't exactly sure he really liked her—but then she wasn't sure she liked him either. What he liked about her was how hard she worked and the way she came up with answers to the tricky questions he liked to throw at people. And what she liked about him was—well, his study, for one thing. He had a lot of other assets, but most of them she had mixed feelings about. Like his high-powered smile and the super-confident manner that made everything he did—even ordinary things like cutting up a steak or walking across the room—seem like highly technical skills. But there was nothing mixed about her feelings concerning real mahogany paneling, a Dutch tiled fireplace, huge leather chairs and an overall atmosphere of unplanned perfection.

"Hey, Summer." Oriole's voice penetrated the flimsy door easily. "Aren't you finished yet? Sparrow's going to sleep."

She put the letters back in the chest and locked it before she opened the door. On the lounge, two thicknesses of foam rubber covered with dirty pillows, Sparrow and Oriole were cuddled together. Their curly red heads were touching—Oriole's pale and flyaway and Sparrow's crisp and chestnut.

Sparrow grunted and yawned and started to get up, but Oriole pulled her back to snuggle—kissing her on both ears and the tip of her nose. Sparrow struggled, playing she didn't like it, but she was grinning, and she finally relented enough to hug Oriole back. But by then she was wide awake again and fussing for a fairy tale before she went to sleep. She'd been hung up on fairy tales lately, particularly ones about princesses.

"Can you read her a fairy tale, baby?" Oriole asked, but Summer shook her head.

"You woke her up," she said. "I didn't."

"Okay," Oriole said. "The snuggle was worth it." She picked Sparrow up and kissed her again. "What'll it be, baby?"

When they'd disappeared into the bedroom, Summer opened the door and went out on the step. The wind was blowing, and she turned her face into it, letting it blow away the anger. Anger at Oriole for pretending that games and kisses were enough, and at Sparrow for not realizing yet that they weren't. Or maybe at herself for a moment's yearning for the long ago time when Oriole's make-believe had been enough for her too.

47

4

Turning the corner on the way to Pardell's class the next afternoon, Summer ran into Haley. "Hey," Haley said, "you missed a real gnarly one."

"A gnarly what?" Summer asked before she remembered about the beach party. "Oh, the beach thing. How'd you make out?"

"Outrageous. Too bad you missed it. Everybody was there."

"Who were you with?"

"Me? Oh, Brownwood, mostly. Janet and I were just bopping around at first, but I wound up with Brownwood."

"Barry Brownwood?" Summer let her surprise show. As far as she was concerned Brownwood was a Grade A lumphead and about a million miles out of Haley's class. Where was Kid?"

Haley's laugh was exaggeratedly unconcerned. "Oh you know the Alvarro shuffle. Kid was with Abbie Norcross."

Summer rolled her eyes. "Wow! How old is she now? About twelve?"

"Thirteen. Thirteen is old enough."

Summer shrugged. Abbie Norcross was an only child with very old-fashioned parents, but she was also very cute. With Kid around, the poor old Norcrosses' ancient ethics didn't stand a chance. "How'd she manage to get out?"

"I helped. I called Mama Norcross and said a bunch of girls were coming to our house for a girl-type party."

"Just a natural born do-gooder," Summer said. She meant her smile to be ambiguous, but the sarcasm must have leaked through because Haley didn't like it.

"What's eating you?" she said coldly.

"Oh, I don't know. I'm just not a Christopher groupie, I guess."

"Well, don't get lonely," Haley said, "because everybody else is. Everybody!"

"Yeah, I know, but what I don't know is—why?"

Haley took the question seriously. So seriously that there weren't any of the new-wave expressions, for which she was famous, in her answer. "Why," she repeated. She thought for a moment with her eyes getting intense and glittery. "It's just that—I guess it's because he just doesn't care. I mean, about anything." Her eyes stopped jittering then, and her voice was cool as she asked, "Do you know what I mean, McIntyre?"

But just at that moment Pardell came around the

corner followed by half the class, which was just as well since what Summer was about to say wasn't very diplomatic. Because she'd suddenly realized why she'd never been anxious to join Christopher's harem. Why, in fact, the one time she'd really had a chance to join the "Blanket Blotchers," when Kid had cornered her behind the bleachers after a game, she'd punched him where it would do the most good—and then ran. The thing was—she'd met him too often before. Haley, with her banker father and PTA president mother, thought Kid Christopher was something absolutely unique; but growing up with Oriole McIntyre you knew better. Guys who didn't care about anything were the story of Oriole's life. And after a few of them traded your last food stamps for pot and hit you with their handmade belts, they didn't seem all that charming anymore.

The class was about Mark Twain that day. There had been an assignment about Twain's use of irony, and Pardell read sections from some of the papers and asked the class to comment on them. He didn't identify the writers, which was just as well, since some of the stuff was pretty stupid. But for the most part, he read things he liked. Summer could tell from some of his comments that he was looking for several of the examples that she had mentioned in her paper, so she felt sure he would read hers, but he never did. That surprised her a little because Pardell usually liked the way she wrote, but she didn't really begin to worry until, as he was dismissing the class, he asked her to stay.

Haley grinned and whispered, "What'd you do,

50

22568

McIntyre? Turn in some pornography?" but no one else paid any attention. Pardell often asked people to stay to talk about their work. But Summer began to feel definitely uneasy. While Pardell was carrying on as usual—blocking the door while he checked his watch to be sure the elderly and infirm had had time to get off the streets, etc., etc—she started looking through her binder. She was sure she'd turned in the assignment; but if she hadn't, it should still be there. It was then she realized what had happened, and, at first, all she could think of doing was jumping up and running out and never coming back. The essay on Mark Twain was right there in the binder pocket; what was missing was a letter to Grant.

She'd finished the letter during her free period, and it was almost the same length as the essay; somehow she must have gotten them mixed up. The first part of the letter had been like a short story. A kind of a-day-in-the-life-of account of one Sunday when the sun had been shining and Oriole had rescued a baby bird, and she and Sparrow had made up a song about it, and Oriole had planned a picnic lunch. But then it had started to rain and the picnic was off. Big disappointment—so Sparrow went to her bedroom and cried, and Oriole went to hers and got stoned. And there was quite a bit more about Sparrow and Oriole and how much alike they were, and how the things that made you want to hug a cute, dopey, helpless seven year old made you want to scream at someone who was supposed to be an adult, not to mention a mother. "I scream at Oriole a lot lately," she'd written, "even though I know it's too late for

51

her to change. It's too late for Oriole and in a different way, it's probably too late for me, and pretty soon now it's going to be too late for Sparrow." It was a ridiculous letter, and she'd known it while she was writing it. There wasn't anything she'd ever written that she'd hate so much for anyone to see. Anyone— even Pardell. Or, maybe, most of all Pardell.

When the last kid had filed out the door, she was standing by his desk with the Mark Twain paper in her hand.

"Here," she said putting it down in front of him. "Here's the assignment. I turned in that other thing by mistake. Can I have it back now? I don't want to talk about it."

"Hey, wait a minute." Pardell said. "Take it easy. You're intimidating me." She went on frowning while he pretended to take his pulse. "See there," he said. "One hundred, at least." He shook his head. "Wow! Clippety clop." As soon as she smiled, he jumped up and got a chair, and the next thing she knew she was sitting down. "Well," he said, "let me see the Mark Twain, then."

He read it through quickly, chuckling now and then and rubbing his hand over the bald spot on top of his head. "Good," he said. "Good. Nice observation." And then, when he had finished, "I like your point about sarcasm rather than irony. A nice distinction. I've noticed that about your writing before, Summer. You use words with a great deal of precision."

But she wasn't about to be deterred from her

objective. "Thanks," she said. "Could I have my letter back now, Mr. Pardell?"

He shuffled through the stack of papers, pulled one out and folded it over, but then he just sat there holding it, even after she held out her hand.

"And sometimes," he said, "you write like a poet —with power and clarity and—" He paused for a moment. "Who's Grant?"

It was a trick Pardell had. She'd seen him use it before. When he talked to just one person, he could make you feel as if what you were saying was the most important thing in the whole world. And even though it was just one of Pardell's tricks, it had worked with her before and it did this time, too. Only a moment before she would have sworn that there wasn't an ice-cube-in-hell's chance that she was going to say anything at all about Grant or the letter; but then Pardell did that perfect listener thing with his big messed-up face, and all of a sudden she heard herself saying, "My father. Grant is my father."

His eyes didn't even flicker, and after a moment he just nodded very slightly and said, "Of course. Of course."

It all came out then—the words welling up from some strange place over which she had no control. "I write to him a lot—for years and years—ever since I learned how to write. Only I don't mail them because I don't know where he is. I don't even know who he is, really. I never saw him. All I know is that Oriole says he was different. He was just hanging out in Carmel like everyone else was then, but with

53

him it was just for that one summer because then he was going back east to go to medical school. Then he met Oriole, and they started traveling together. Oriole didn't know she was pregnant until after he went away. She never wrote to him about it because she didn't want him to come back and mess up his life. And then she lost the address. So I just write to him and keep the letters in a box. There's a lot of them now—hundreds, maybe."

She'd been looking down at the desk as she talked, rubbing at a spot where ink had soaked into the wood—rubbing hard as if she could scrub it away. Her voice was a little shaky, but her eyes were all right until she looked up and saw the expression on Pardell's face; that was when she began to cry. She fought it for a moment, frowning and clenching her teeth, but her throat swelled shut and tears burned in her eyes and finally she gave up and put her head down on the desk.

While she was crying, Pardell didn't do or say anything; but when she began to stop, he got up and went to the back of the room and wet a paper towel in the sink and brought it to her. She wiped her face and gathered up her things without looking at him; but when she started for the door, he went with her. He stopped with one hand on the doorknob, holding it shut. When she looked up at him, he just nodded, narrow-eyed, as if he were sizing her up. "I'm sorry," he said. "But I'm a lot sorrier for this Grant character than I am for you. He doesn't even know what he's been missing." Then he opened the door and let her out.

Most of the way home she stumbled along in a blinding storm of angry humiliation. Ignoring Sparrow's chatter, she listened only to a litany of phrases, which kept repeating themselves like a broken record inside her head. "How could I be so stupid—stupid to hand in that letter—stupid to write it in the first place—stupid to write to someone who doesn't exist. And, most unbearable of all—stupid to have cried in front of Pardell. For no reason! There was nothing to cry about. Nothing had changed. Everything was just the way it had always been—and she hadn't cried for years and years.

It wasn't until they reached the first redwood grove that she began to calm down enough to look at what had happened from some other points of view. She'd noticed that about redwoods. There was something about them—their size and age maybe—that made you realize a lot of small miserable things just didn't matter very much. She'd stood there before, looking up at their beauty and their slow, patient strength, and whatever it was that had been churning around inside her suddenly felt small and hushed. So, because of the redwoods or for whatever reason, she began to realize that there was one consolation. At least she knew that Pardell wouldn't tell anyone about what had happened. She didn't know how she knew, but she did. And there was what he'd said about her writing. She couldn't help feeling good about that. And what he'd said at the end about Grant's not knowing what he'd been missing. It didn't make a whole lot of sense, actually, but for some reason it made her feel quite a bit better.

By the time they'd reached the second grove, she'd cheered up enough to register a little of what Sparrow had been trying to tell her about a movie on the evils of smoking that she'd seen at school. Still thinking about Pardell—that he might never mention it again, and she certainly wouldn't mention it, and it would almost be as if it hadn't happened—she was halfway listening to Sparrow rattle on about how bad smoking was for people.

"Is smoking pot as bad as cigarettes?" Sparrow was asking. "Do people who smoke pot get those sores inside them, too? Summer! What's the matter with you? Why won't you talk to me?"

"Nothing's the matter," Summer said. Sparrow's soft round face was puckered into a worried frown. Summer grinned at her. "Nothing's the matter, Funny-face. Come on. I'll race you to the turn-off."

When they arrived home a few breathless minutes later, they found Galya there. Sitting cross-legged on the foam rubber, she and Oriole were drinking peppermint tea and talking nonstop, the same as always. Nonstop, at least, until they heard footsteps on the stairs—and broke off abruptly.

Galya got her tongue going again first. "Hi kids. Come here and give us a smooch." She held out her arms with their jangly bracelets. She looked the same as she always had—homespun skirt, peasant blouse, sandals—except that recently her outfits, while still hippie style, were more craftshop-expensive instead of homemade-cheap. But her gray streaked hair was still long and loose and her hands were as garden-rough as ever.

Sparrow flung herself into Galya's arms. "How's my favorite production?" Galya crooned as she snuggled Sparrow, kissing her on both cheeks. "How's my beautiful redheaded masterpiece?" Galya always made a big thing out of the fact that she'd midwifed Sparrow's birth, claiming that made Sparrow partly hers.

Sparrow hugged back for only a moment before she pushed away. "Is Marina back?" she asked. "She is, isn't she? Didn't Marina come back home?"

Galya and Oriole exchanged quick glances. The flick of Galya's eyes was ambiguous, but as usual, Oriole's face was an open book. The sneaky guilt of her expression was about as hard to miss as a thunderclap. Summer hoped that if they were going to lie to Sparrow, Galya would be the one to do it. Watching Oriole lie was a maddening mixture of anger and humiliation.

"No, baby," Galya said, trying to hug Sparrow to her—to comfort her, or perhaps, to avoid having to meet her eyes. "We hope it won't be too much longer before she can come home. But you know, it's a lot warmer and drier in Lodi, and it's better for Marina there."

She went on for quite a while about how much better Marina's wheeze was and how much she was missing Sparrow and what her new school was like— and Summer listened wondering how she could be so convincing if she were making it up. Oriole's face might have been an indication—but she'd gotten up to make some more tea and was standing over the stove with her back turned. Even when Sparrow began about finding the troll doll, Galya's answers were smooth and quick. "It must have been there all along, sweetie," she said, "and you just didn't happen to notice it. I'm sure that must be it." She turned to Summer as if she'd been reading her suspicious thoughts. "I'm sure that was it. Don't you think so, Summer?"

"Oh sure," Summer said, but she was less sure now than a moment before, mostly because Galya was giving her a level-eyed super-sincere expression that suddenly reminded her of the time Galya had told them about how she'd gotten Jerry to marry her.

The problem had been that neither Jerry or Galya had believed in marriage when they first met, but after they'd had three kids and Galya had inherited the land and started the organic farming business, she'd changed her mind. She knew Jerry well enough to know that if she came right out and said so, it would only make him more against the whole idea. So for months she had come down to see Oriole and report on her latest schemes and strategies to get Jerry to change his mind. Sometimes she'd act it out, taking both parts in the arguments and conversations in which she would come out strongly against marriage so that Jerry would be trapped into taking the opposite point of view. It was a technique that worked very well on Jerry, Galya said, because, like most men, he specialized in opposite points of view.

"It's just that I can't see myself making promises about how I'm going to feel ten years from now," she would say—acting out how she'd said it to Jerry

—and there would be that very same super-sincere expression on her broad dark-eyed face.

Obviously Galya was conning somebody again, but this time it was the McIntyres, or at least Summer and Sparrow. All of which made it look even more probable that something weird was going on at the Fishers'. And for some reason, whatever it was was related to Marina's absence. That brought the whole thing closer to home, because whatever affected Marina was going to involve Sparrow to some extent. And that made it Summer's business, whether she wanted it to be or not.

5

She heard the peacocks screaming as soon as she stepped off the bus. Partway up the hill she came across a bunch of them in the middle of the drive—three males and several of the much less colorful but no less proud and arrogant females. One of the males was parading in a circle with his tail fanned in an enormous halo of quivering plumes. The others, definitely unimpressed, went on about their business, but Summer couldn't help stopping for a moment to watch.

They'd fascinated her since her first day at Crown Ridge when she'd come across a flock of them stalking haughtily across the lawn in front of the long, low house—creatures from some pagan paradise, their incredibly gorgeous plumage in strange contrast to the weird reptilian movement of their gaudy heads and dragon-clawed legs. Even now, after finding out how dumb and neurotic and basically useless they were, she still found them intriguing and somehow, even more than the Arabians, a very important part of the whole scene at Crown Ridge Ranch.

She stood motionless, watching the preening strut of the big male until he lowered his gigantic fan and wandered off among the shrubbery. Then she picked up a couple of fallen plumes and hurried on up the drive.

Nan was still eating her breakfast when Summer knocked on the back door. She was wearing her quilted velvet dressing gown, and her long pale hair was looped at the back of her neck in a loose chignon. As always, she looked as classy and perfectly groomed as one of her horses. While Summer unloaded her backpack—two boxes of strawberries and some to-matoes from the Fisher greenhouses—Nan went back to her coffee and croissants at the breakfast table.

"Oh, marvelous," she said when she saw the straw-berries. "Just what this breakfast needed. Would you give them a little wash and put them in one of the blue bowls. Just one box for now. That will be lovely."

Of course Galya had already washed the berries, but Summer didn't argue. When they were all care-fully rewashed and arranged in the bowl, she took them to the table.

"Thank you, dear. They're beautiful. They look like a painting in that bowl, don't they?" Nan said. Then she smiled her wide, even-toothed smile. "Now sit down for a moment." Summer sat down and smiled back. Nan's gaze was warm, approving and concerned —very much the way it was when she looked at her

61

Arabians. "Did you eat before you came this morning," she asked, and when Summer shook her head, "You really shouldn't go without breakfast, dear. You're much too thin."

"I wasn't hungry," Summer said, "and besides there wasn't—" She stopped, shrugging. But Nan saw the shrug and asked, "There wasn't what?"

"Oh nothing. About the strawberries—Galya said to tell you she'd have more next Saturday. Bigger ones."

"That will be lovely, but these are quite nice. Amazing really, for this early in the year. Now you just jump up and get a plate and some silverware and have a few of these berries and some nice hot croissants before you start to work. No, don't argue. You'll get ever so much more done on a full stomach."

Summer hadn't intended to argue. There wasn't much point with Nan, particularly when it came to being fed. Richard, who had the beginnings of a pot belly, sometimes made comments about Nan's nurturing compulsion. According to him, Nan force fed everything that came within reach. Actually, he wasn't far wrong. Nearly everything at Crown Ridge looked slightly pudgy, from Richard right on down: eleven Arabians not counting the colts, two dogs, four cats, six canaries and about a dozen peacocks. And judging by the amount of plant food Nan was always doling out, even her African violets were probably overweight.

There were, however, definite limits to Nan's nurturing instincts. During their many discussions, usually held over one table or another, Summer had

62

learned that Nan disapproved of feeding people when it was done by governments or institutions. She was very much against food stamps and school lunch programs, and she even wondered if feeding starving people in other countries didn't ultimately do more harm than good. "Richard and I are sorry for hungry people, of course," she'd told Summer more than once, "but we believe that giving people food takes away their freedom and initiative."

That was another thing Summer didn't argue with Nan about. Actually, in some ways she agreed. Nobody could possibly hate food stamps as much as she did—but at the same time she was pretty sure that she and Sparrow would have starved to death several times over while Oriole was developing the initiative she might have been capable of if her food stamps had been taken away.

So Summer just listened and watched, and it didn't take long to figure out that Nan's food dispensing behavior was only triggered by mouths that, in one way or another, belonged to her. And when she began to insist on feeding Summer, it seemed to indicate that she was thinking of Summer as one of her possessions. It was a concept to which Summer had given a certain amount of thought.

As soon as she'd eaten enough strawberries and croissants to satisfy Nan, she got to work. As usual, she began with the kitchen. Scrubbing a kitchen, even one like Nan's with its sleek tile surfaces and gleaming appliances, was still pretty much your basic everyday drudgery. She worked hard and fast to get it over with and get on to the rooms she really enjoyed.

It was almost eleven o'clock and the master bedroom was nearly finished when Nan came into the room. Summer was dusting a picture, the small one in the silver frame that always sat on the night stand, and when Nan saw what she was doing something frightening happened to her face. For a moment Summer wondered if she could have been told not to touch the picture and had somehow forgotten, but then she realized that what was written on Nan's face wasn't anger after all. She waited, holding the picture carefully with both hands, as Nan came slowly around the bed, took it away from her and just stood looking at it for a long time before she said anything.

It was a photograph of a little girl about six or seven years old wearing an English riding outfit and sitting on a small pony. Summer had noticed the photo many times because the girl with her round-eyed face and thick pigtails reminded her of Sparrow. But now, looking more closely at the short-nosed, wide-mouthed face, she suddenly realized that there was a definite resemblance to Nan.

"You?" she asked. "When you were little?"

Nan shook her head. "No," she said. "This is Deborah. My little girl." Although she had said is not was, Summer knew immediately that Deborah was dead. Nan's face said so, and so did the throb in her voice. Summer waited, and after a moment Nan went on. "She died of leukemia a few months after this picture was taken."

Summer's voice wavered when she said, "I'm sorry" and Nan reached out and squeezed her hand;

but what had made Summer's throat tighten really had very little to do with Nan and the dead Deborah. Mostly it was because of Sparrow who was the same age and even got the same funny expression on her face when her picture was being taken.

At lunch that day, while Nan was making sure that Summer ate every crumb of an enormous crab salad sandwich, she went on talking about Deborah— about what an exceptional child she had been, bright and beautiful and happy—and about the diagnosis of leukemia and the terrible months that followed. After it was over, Nan said, she had gone into a state of deep depression that lasted for many months.

"That's why we're here, actually," she told Summer. "I'd always wanted to raise Arabians, and Richard thought it would be good for me. A change of scene and something to occupy my mind. So when he heard about this place, he bought it, and we sold our home in Connecticut and moved out. Richard was already spending as much time on the West Coast as on the East, so it made very little difference as far as our time together was concerned. I was terribly busy at first with the remodeling and finding good breeding stock, and after a while it did help."

"You never had any other children?" Summer asked.

"No. There were some serious problems when Deborah was born and eventually an operation. I wasn't able to have any more children."

Summer gathered up her dishes and Nan's and took them to the dishwasher, where she stood for a moment staring out of the window and down the long

65

sweep of lawn to where the peacocks were passing in ceremonial procession. But this time their weird prehistoric posturing was depressing—sinister almost, like some strange inhuman ritual for the dead. She turned her eyes away. Later, as she was sponging off the table, she asked Nan if she'd ever thought about adopting a baby.

Nan sighed. "Actually I did," she said, "but Richard wouldn't hear of it. His parents adopted a baby boy before he was born and it turned out tragically. Jeffrey, his adoptive brother, turned out very badly. He died, eventually, in an automobile accident, drunk driving, and Richard's parents nearly impoverished themselves to take care of the hospital bills—his and the other people involved in the accident. It all happened years ago, but it left Richard absolutely opposed to adoption. Nothing I could say, no examples of successful adoptions, made any difference."

The half-hour Summer usually allowed herself for lunch was over long before Nan stopped talking. Every time Summer tried to get back to work, Nan made her sit back down to hear a little more. When it was finally over, she understood a lot of things about the Olivers that she hadn't before, but she was also a long way behind on her work. It was almost time for her bus and she was only starting the study when Nan came into the room.

"Here," she said, handing Summer her check. "It's for the full amount. It was my fault you didn't finish. You run along now and catch your bus. We'll just skip the rest of the house this week." She stopped, looked around the study, and ran her finger along the edge of a bookshelf. "Unless you could come back tomorrow morning." She smiled her wide smile. "Would that be possible, dear?"

Summer said that it would.

When she got back to the trailer, Cerbe was tied up and Sparrow was home alone. She was sitting at the kitchen table drawing pictures, and she jumped up when Summer came in.

"Hi." she said. "Hi, Summer. Did you bring me a peacock feather? Did you get to feed the horses today? How are they? How are the horses? Are there any new baby ones?"

Summer hung her backpack on the hook by the door. "Where's Oriole? she asked.

"She went into town with Angelo to go shopping. She said they were going to get bananas and raisins and everything. And you know what, Summer? Cerbe was very bad, and that's why he's tied up."

"Did she say when she was coming home?" Summer said.

"You know what Cerbe did? He tried to bite Angelo. And Angelo had to climb up the madrone tree and yell for Oriole to come and get him. And Oriole spanked Cerbe and tied him up, and he's supposed to stay there until she gets back and . . ." Sparrow stopped babbling and stared at Summer.

The anger wasn't at Sparrow, but she obviously felt it. Watching Summer warily, she climbed back into her chair. "She said she wouldn't be gone long," she offered hopefully. "She'll probably be back real soon."

Summer took the stuff out of her backpack and slammed it down on the table so hard that Sparrow jumped as if she'd been slapped. Then she turned and stalked out and right down to the end of the trailer where Cerbe was tied. Watching her approach, he performed his ritual welcome dance, bouncing around in circles and then crouching in a kind of bow, with his curly tail waving like a frenzied football fan's banner. When she squatted down in front of him, he gamboled around her, tangling them both in his rope until she toppled over. She lay on her back covering her face with her arms to protect it from his kisses until he got tired and collapsed beside her, his chin on her shoulder. Reaching over she took hold of his muzzle with two fingers and lifted his floppy lips to reveal the long sharp canines. "I wish you had," she whispered fiercely. "I wish you'd bitten his leg off." When she got up, she untied Cerbe and took him with her into the trailer.

Oriole did come home fairly soon that day, but after that she started being away more and more often. At first she offered a variety of flimsy excuses, but after a while she said she had a job.

"I'm working for the Fishers," she said. "I'm helping them plant the new greenhouses that Angelo and Bart built."

That left several questions without answers. Like —how long it took eight people—four Fishers, three weirdos and Oriole, to plant three greenhouses. And there was also another question that wasn't asked or answered, and that was just what it was that the Fishers were planting. Summer was afraid to ask that one. Afraid, first of all that Oriole would lie to her, and even more afraid of what the answer might be if, by some chance, she decided to tell the truth. So she kept her suspicions strictly to herself. She didn't even write to Grant about it.

She hadn't, in fact, written to Grant for almost three weeks. Not since the day she'd had the disaster with Pardell. It was possible that she never would anymore. Not that she'd made any definite decision about it, because she hadn't. However writing to a nonexistent person was a habit one might be expected to outgrow at some point, and it was beginning to look as if that time had come.

Then on May thirty-first Oriole stayed out all night; and when she strolled in at eight-thirty in the morning, Summer yelled at her and there was another violent argument. That night Summer wrote to Grant again.

She said she'd worked late and decided to spend the night at the Fishers', and all I said was, "With who?" and she got mad and said I was worse than her parents used to be and that she didn't see how she could have produced such an up-tight hung-up kid, and if she'd known how I was going to turn out she would have abandoned me on the doorstep of some stuffy Orange County reactionaries. So I said, no, she wouldn't, because she'd never had enough money for a ticket to Orange County in her whole life, and she said that's what it was all about, wasn't it? Money!!! That's what she always says when we fight. That I'm really angry at her because she doesn't have "a legally wedded sugar daddy with a high-salaried nine-to-five job and a ticky-tacky split-level house and all the rest of the establishment crap." There's no use arguing with her when she gets on that kick so I just came in here and locked the door.

But that's not it. It's not money that I want. At least, it's not just money. I want a lot more than that. What I want is—something else, but whatever it is, it's not here. And as soon as I get a chance I'm going to get the hell out of Alvarro Bay and go looking for it.

The next day Oriole was cringingly conciliatory. Summer despised her for it, and herself for causing it. The whole scene was giving her a stomachache, so she said she was sorry and Oriole looked delighted and said she was sorry too and why didn't the three of them go into town and see if they could find somebody who would trade some food stamps for enough money to buy three tickets to *Superman II*. Sparrow jumped up and down and yelled, "Goody! Goody!" but Summer said, "Thanks just the same but I'd prefer to skip it, unless you can get Superman to keep us from having to live on stale bread for two days like we did last month."

So Oriole said, "Okay, forget it." But afterwards Summer was sorry she hadn't taken her up on the offer because Oriole went out by herself and didn't come back until almost morning, and after that she quit trying to cover up and make excuses. Just like always, when she had a new man, she forgot about everybody and everything else. She was away from home most of the time; and when she was there, she was always listening for the sound of the pickup's horn blaring away—two shorts and two longs—from way out on the road.

It had happened before with Danny and Mike and Jim and Rif and etc., but this time there was one difference. The others had all spent a lot of time at the trailer, even the ones who never actually moved in; but this new one, this Angelo creep, never came any closer than the end of the path. At least not since Cerbe chased him up the madrone. That was one thing, Summer supposed, she had to be thankful for, and it was obviously Cerbe who got the credit.

At school things had been all right. Facing Pardell again after the fiasco about the letter hadn't been easy; but he'd never mentioned it in any way, and after a while she stopped watching to see if he was going to treat her any differently. If anything had changed at all, it was just that she thought she noticed more times when he did his "private message" bit with her, catching her eye when something was significant or funny—like the time he asked if anyone had read "The Highway Man," and Brownwood said he'd read the first few chapters.

Summer turned sixteen on the last day of the month, and that was a change for the better. It seemed like growing up had been taking forever, and she'd

71

been anxious to get on with it for as long as she could remember. There was another small change for the better, too, during that last month of school. Sparrow finally quit begging to go to the Fishers'. At first when Oriole started going there every day, Sparrow wanted to go along, but after a while she had given up. The fierce dog and Jerry's bad mood and even Angelo and Bart hadn't discouraged her, but what did make a difference was the fact that Oriole, who was now in a position to know, said that Marina had not come home—and Sparrow believed her.

Summer was glad she no longer had to watch Sparrow to keep her from sneaking off up the hill; but at the same time it worried her a little that, at the age of seven, Sparrow still believed everything Oriole said. At seven Summer had already known better for quite a while.

6

Rose early and off down the road to catch the early coach. The weather, which has been unseasonably cold, has turned fine, and I greatly enjoyed the brief communion with nature that the walk provided. Having arrived at my place of employment, I set about my customary duties and the day progressed normally until, during my noontime repast, when my employer . . ."

"Okay! Okay Cerbe! Come find me."

Cerbe, who had been sitting obediently at the foot of the trailer steps with his head cocked and his ears twitching, leaped to his feet and dashed around the corner. A moment later there was a sharp bark, a delighted squeal and Sparrow appeared, skipping happily with Cerbe gamboling beside her. "He found me. He found me, Summer. I was hiding behind the watertank, and he just sniffed right across the yard and found me, as quick as anything." She threw her arms around the dog's neck and hugged him so enthusiastically she tipped them both over. On his back, with his big feet waving in the air, Cerbe growled with mock ferocity, grabbed Sparrow's skinny little arm in his huge jaws and held it very gently while she squealed with excitement.

"Look, Summer. Cerbe's biting me. Don't you want to see how Cerbe's biting me?"

Summer sighed. "Do I have a choice?" she said. Closing her binder and putting her pen behind her ear, she leaned back against the trailer's screen door and turned her full attention to the dusty battle at her feet. "You're getting filthy," she said mildly.

"I know." Sparrow got to her feet and made an ineffectual attempt to dust off her jeans. "Hide-and-go seek is a filthy game. What are you writing, Summer?"

"Nothing. I'm not writing anything. I gave up. It's hard to write at a wrestling match." Actually, she hadn't stopped just because of the noisy game. If she were really into writing, it took more than Sparrow's chatter to spoil her concentration. Part of it was probably the weather. "What is so rare as a day in June," Pardell had recited last week on the first day of June; and today was another rare one—soft and green and golden, and so alive with growth you could almost hear it. Lifting her face to the sun, she closed her eyes and let her mind drift. The writing could wait. She wasn't going to turn it in anyway.

Pardell had given the assignment, an extra credit one for people who needed to improve their grade, in connection with a project on journal writers. He'd started by reading excerpts from the writings of

74

people like Franklin and Pepys and Boswell, and then he'd had everyone write a paragraph in the style of one of the diarists. He read some of those paragraphs, and everyone had guessed which famous journal-keeper the writer had been trying to imitate. The extra credit assignment was to keep a journal about the events of the following week. Since she didn't need the grade, Summer hadn't intended to do it—until the week turned out to be one of the most important of her entire life. It had all begun at noon on Saturday.

She had sensed a difference as soon as she walked into the Ranch kitchen. Nan was at the table and, as usual, she insisted that Summer join her, but she seemed quieter than usual as if something was on her mind. It wasn't until lunchtime that it all came out. They were eating their chicken salad and bran muffins at the wrought iron table in the patio when Nan suddenly said, "Well, we've had an exciting time around here since last weekend. Richard came home last Tuesday with some incredible news and by Thursday we'd made the decision. We're going back to Connecticut."

"Going back to Connecticut?" Summer said. "But what about . . ." What she was really thinking was, "What about my bank account?" but what she said was, "What about the horses?"

"If we can find a place with a stable, I'll probably take Scimitar and Greybird with me, but I'm afraid we'll have to sell the others. You see, there's been a decision to enlarge the New York plant, and Richard will have to be there full time for at least a year.

75

Now that I've made the decision, I feel very good about it. California has been good for us but our roots are back East—family and many old friends. But we'll miss this place tremendously—and the horses and all our special California friends." She reached out and put her big smooth hand with its heavy rings over Summer's. "We're going to miss you, my dear. As a matter of fact, Richard and I were discussing the possibility of taking you with us."

"With you?" This time there was absolutely no pretense in Summer's reaction—her astonishment was real and complete. "But . . . but . . ." she stammered and then, stupidly, "Clear to Connecticut? But where would I live?"

"Why, with us, of course. Summer, dear . . ." Nan leaned forward, and her smile said she was going to talk about something personal.

Summer felt herself tensing. She knew that kind of smile—smugly sympathetic. People had smiled at her like that before, and it usually meant they were getting ready to say something about Oriole. Not kids so much. Some kids thought there would be advantages to living with a mother like Oriole. But adults usually mentioned Oriole in the same tone of voice they used when there'd been a death in the family or someone had come down with an incurable disease.

"We've made some discreet inquiries, dear," Nan said. "Of course we'd heard rumors before, but we wanted to know a bit more about your background."

Summer managed to control her face, but as usual her body betrayed her—stiffening and pulling away.

Nan smiled understandingly. "Don't worry," she said. "It doesn't change our opinion of you in the slightest. In fact, quite the contrary. We think you deserve even more credit than we'd realized. Richard kept saying that it reminded him of his Grandfather Mahoney's story—a case of God-given gumption against all odds. What we've been thinking is that we'd just continue as we have here, except that you'd be living in, which would mean that you could spread the work out and do a bit every day after school instead of just on Saturdays." Nan's smile was wide-screen benevolent. "I know," she said. "You must be feeling quite overwhelmed. You don't need to decide right away. We won't even be putting the house on the market for several weeks, so in the meantime we'll go on just as before. But you think about it, won't you?"

Summer said she would. She thought about it all the rest of the day while she dusted the gleaming furniture and vacuumed the deep soft rugs and swept the peacock droppings off the patio. And the more she thought about it, the angrier she became. Nan's unspoken comments about Oriole made her angry, and the "discreet inquiries" made her angrier, and the "God-given gumption" made her angriest of all. But before she went home that afternoon, when she told Nan good-by, she gave her a sincere, serious smile and said she was still thinking about it.

That much was true. She had thought about nothing else all afternoon, and on the way home she was still thinking about it. But what wasn't true was the implication that she was undecided. Not that there

77

weren't aspects of Nan's offer that intrigued her. She had to admit to that and even to a long-standing fantasy in which she was, in some vague, undefined way, a part of the Oliver's peacock world. But the part she'd envisioned herself playing in that world was not that of live-in maid and certainly not in Connecticut—three thousand miles away from Sparrow and Oriole. Her answer would be no. All that remained was how to say it so that the Olivers wouldn't be angry. She wanted to keep the job as long as possible.

That had been the first event that had made the past week one that almost demanded to be recorded, and the second one took place only a few days later. It began with Pardell asking her to stay after class again. Even though there was no reason that she could think of and certainly no possibility of another misplaced letter, she had been uneasy. As she waited for the rest of the class to file out, she could feel the fluttery tightness beginning in her stomach.

"Well," Pardell said, when the other students had all gone, "don't look so apprehensive. There's no problem. It's just that I'm about to offer you a summer job."

"A job," she repeated blankly, wiped out by surprise.

"Right. You see, Meg, my wife, is due to go into the hospital in about two weeks. Nothing serious, just an old knee injury that's been giving her some trouble recently. But she'll be in a wheelchair and then on crutches for quite a while, which wouldn't present any problem except that I'm committed to a summer school stint in Fort Bragg. So we're going to need someone to stay with her while I'm away and help out around the house. Perhaps you already have plans for the summer but . . ." He broke off as Summer began to nod.

"Yes," she said. "Yes, I'd like the job, that is. And no, I don't have any other plans. That is, I do have a job already but it's only for weekends, so I could be at your place during the week."

Pardell said that was great, and they set up a time for Summer to go over to talk to his wife, and that was it. It wasn't until she was halfway home that she realized he must have decided to ask her if she wanted the job because of that letter to Grant. There'd been a part in it about her bank account and the job at Crown Ridge Ranch—which obviously was the reason Pardell knew she was into doing housework. It was a disturbing thought. But at least he hadn't mentioned what had given him the idea. Because if he had mentioned it, she would have had to turn him down.

Then, two days later, there had been the interview with Meg Pardell. Summer had gone to the house, a small Victorian on the north edge of the village, after picking Sparrow up at the elementary school. She made Sparrow wait for her in the front yard while she went in. She'd known Meg Pardell by sight for a long time—everyone in Alvarro Bay knew everyone else by sight—a small thin woman with a pixie haircut; but it was the first time they'd ever spoken. She turned out to be easy to talk to.

She led the way into the living room chattering

away about how great it was that Summer was going to be able to help them out. "I know you'll do a wonderful job," she said, smiling in a way that made it easy to smile back.

"How do you know that?" Summer asked. "Because I'm getting an A in English? I've heard that lots of writers are real slobs."

"That's probably true. But I wasn't basing my expectations on just your English grade. You just seem to me to be the kind of person who does a lot of things well. As a matter of fact, I've heard as much. Such information is common knowledge in the school community, you know. By the time a student gets to be your age in a town this small, he or she has been discussed by a lot of teachers—not to mention teachers' wives and husbands. The rumor is you're a very competent kid. How about some apple cider?"

"Oh yeah?" Summer said, intrigued. The part about talk and rumors in a small town was certainly true, and teachers probably talked as much or more than anyone else. But she doubted the rest of it. She suspected that when teachers talked about the McIntyre kids, they were mainly interested in things beside grades and schoolwork. Like Mrs. Boswick, the third grade teacher, who happened to see Mr. Boswick talking to Oriole downtown one day and afterwards kept pumping Summer about the men Oriole was seeing.

"How about some apple cider?" Meg said again.

"What? Oh, yes please." Summer said.

While Meg was in the kitchen, Summer checked out the room. Of medium size, with a high ceiling and long, narrow windows, it was slightly shabby-looking and cluttered with too many bookcases, a huge grand piano, stacks of newspapers and sheet music and various kinds of foreign looking art objects. In spite of the fact that it was much smaller than the Olivers' house, it looked as if the Pardells' might turn out to be a lot more work. But it was also going to be five days a week, and the money was going to make a big difference in the growth rate of the bank account.

When Meg came back with the cider, they discussed hourly rates and a starting date, and then Meg rambled on for quite a while about Jason, the Pardells' son who was working in Washington D.C., and the operation she was going to have on her knee.

"It was injured in an automobile accident years ago," she said, "and it's been bothering me for a long time, but I kept putting off doing anything about it. I hated to leave Alan alone to cope—he's a disaster in the kitchen—and to abandon my students for such a long time." Meg gestured toward the piano. Summer knew about Meg's piano students. Haley had been one of them, and probably Summer, herself, would have been if Oriole could have afforded it. "But it turns out I'll only have to be in the hospital for a few days. Of course, I'll be pretty immobile for a while, but I'll be able to go on teaching. I'm awfully glad we're going to have you here to help. As I said, Alan is absolutely useless around the house, and even if he weren't, he's going to be very busy this summer. There's the summer school, and besides he's had a positive response to one of his queries—on an article

81

he's been wanting to write about the politics of the classroom—and he needs to get in some time at the typewriter."

"An article?" Summer asked. "Does Mr. Pardell write?"

"Yes indeed. He's had several articles and short stories published, and, of course, there's the novel. Or I guess there is. Whenever he's faced with an unpleasant chore, or an uninspiring guest, he retires to his study to work on it; but as far as I know, no one's ever seen it."

They both laughed. "I've heard some stuff he wrote," Summer said. "Sometimes when he's reading assignments, he'll read a really funny one—you know, full of puns and all sorts of crazy mistakes. The first time he did it, everybody was trying to guess who wrote it, but after that we always knew right away when it was one of his."

"That's Alan for you," Meg said. "Instead of working on his great epic, he spends his time writing bad examples for his classes."

When the cider was finished, Summer collected Sparrow, who was sitting patiently on the front steps talking to a big orange cat, and started home—listening to Sparrow's chatter with half her brain while the other half figured out what her weekly and monthly income was going to be, and how much of it she'd be able to put away in the bank.

So—in just one week she'd been offered a new job in Alvarro Bay, a weird kind of foster child/upstairs maid position in Connecticut, not to mention another offer from Nicky—the usual one, in which she was

MASTERMAN I M C

given the opportunity to trade her virginity for a chance to go steady. So far that was the only one she had definitely declined. All in all there had been enough material to fill a sizable journal.

It wasn't until Sparrow lost interest in the game of hide-and-seek and went into the trailer and Cerbe flopped down in the sun to sleep, that Summer took the pen out from behind her ear and began to write. It went quickly, and when she finished and read it over, she thought it was pretty good—Boswell, mostly, with a few touches of Pepys. It was too bad, really, that she couldn't turn it in, but of course she wasn't about to. She couldn't let Pardell read it, or anyone else, for that matter. Suddenly she scratched out the title, A TRUE ACCOUNT OF THE EVENTS IN THE LIFE OF SUMMER MCINTYRE, JUNE 2 TO 9, and in its place wrote, "Dear Grant,". She pulled the key over her head before she went inside.

The last day of school came and went with the usual celebrations, and the next morning Summer got up extra early in time to catch the first bus. Sparrow was still sound asleep. She didn't move when Summer got out of bed, but when Summer tucked the blankets back around her, she sighed deeply and muttered something about Marina. Summer bent close.

Sparrow's face twitched, her head moved from side to side, and once again her lips formed her friend's name. Dreaming again. Just the night before she'd wakened Summer to tell her that Marina had looked in the window again and called her. Summer had had to get up and go with her to look all around the yard before she'd believe it hadn't really hap-

83

pened. Poor kid. Losing Marina was probably only the beginning of a lot of things that would haunt her sleep. Summer waited, watching and listening and noticing the way Sparrow's thick coppery eyelashes fringed her eyelids. She looked shiny and silky soft and new as an unopened Christmas package. When her breathing had become deep and steady again, Summer gathered up her clothing and tiptoed into the living room to dress.

There was no sound from the other bedroom either, but Oriole was there, all right. Summer had heard her come home—around two o'clock in the morning. There was nothing much in the refrigerator except the berries and tomatoes for Nan. It didn't matter much. She'd eat at the Olivers, and there was enough granola for Sparrow's breakfast. What Oriole would eat when she finally got up would be her problem. At least there was plenty of kibble for Cerbe.

She mixed the kibble with water and put it outside near the steps. Cerbe wasn't around and she didn't want to call him for fear of waking Sparrow. He wouldn't be gone long—not at mealtime. There was nothing more to do but load her backpack and start off down the trail through the early morning mist.

It was a strange morning—the thin wispy fog drifting in ghostly veils among the trees, with here and there a slanting ray of sunlight piercing the shadows like a spotlight from another world. As she started down the path toward the Fishers' road, Summer could feel a knot of tension like a clenched fist at the back of her neck, but as she walked through

84

the awakening forest the knot began to unravel. She sighed deeply, breathing out worry and anger and breathing in misty shadows and spicy sun-touched warmth. She increased her pace, striding free and easy toward the road and the bus and Crown Ridge— and the summer that was just beginning. At the end of the path a heap of gray brown fur lay beside the road.

Summer heard a voice that must have been her own say, "Cerbe?" even before the shock wave hit, and then, "Oh no. Cerbe. No." She knelt beside him, and for a brief, desperate moment she told herself that he might be only stunned or injured, but then her hand, slowly and against her will, reached out—and told her it wasn't true. Under the shaggy coat, Cerbe's body was cold and stiff. His jaws gaped open, and beneath his muzzle there was a small pool of dried blood.

Clenching her teeth against a horrible sound that throbbed at the back of her throat, she held herself motionless, her mind blank and empty except for a deep, wordless ache. But when the numbness began to recede, what took its place was anger, and a question—and then more questions. How did it happen? Who had been driving fast on the narrow dirt road— late at night, because Cerbe had been in the trailer until just before she went to bed. And what had he been doing on the road? He never went far from the trailer after dark. And he'd always been so smart about cars. Why hadn't he heard the car and gotten out of the way?

It was then, without knowing what she was looking for, that she began to search. A few feet from where Cerbe was lying she found a spot of blood, and farther down the path, another one. As she moved on —back down the path toward the trailer—the spots were closer together, and then, in the midst of the first clearing, she found where it had happened. Beside the path a larger pool of blood had been partially covered with leaves and pine needles, as if someone had hastily scraped at the ground in a clumsy attempt to hide the evidence—the evidence that Cerbe had died here, at least fifty yards from the road, and then been carried to where it might seem that he had been struck by a car.

The cold hard rage helped in a way, shutting out the grief and pity. Shutting out not only the memory of Cerbe warm and lively and loving, but also any feeling of revulsion for the stiff bloody thing beside the road. With cold efficiency Summer went back and examined the body and confirmed her suspicions beyond the shadow of a doubt. Then she returned to the trailer for a shovel and wheelbarrow.

She dug the grave because of Sparrow. If it hadn't been for Sparrow she would have dumped what was left of Cerbe in front of the door—or on the kitchen floor or on Oriole's bed. That's where she should put it—right on Oriole's bed. Oriole ought not to mind. She ought to be willing to give up her bed for Cerbe since it was her fault he was dead. It wasn't as if it was the only bed she had. Beds were one thing there'd never been any shortage of where Oriole was concerned. Plunging the shovel violently into the soft earth, stomping on it, lifting and throwing the loosened soil, she worked hard and fast—holding on to the anger that was keeping her mind sharp and clear. There was a lot of thinking to be done and plans to be made.

When the grave was finished, she tilted the wheelbarrow, and it was only then—as the big bear-shaped head, the head that had held so much love and joy and loyalty, slid over the edge and hung down above the hole—that she almost lost her hold. But she fought back, crushing down the grief and pity and reaching out for the insulating fury. And when it returned, she carefully covered the grave with earth and then with pine needles and returned the shovel and wheelbarrow to the shed. Then she went in and woke up Sparrow.

"Come on, get up," she said as Sparrow sat up, tousled and groggy. "How would you like to go to work with me today?"

7

"How come you let me come today? Huh? Huh, Summer? How come you let me come with you this time? You always said they wouldn't like it if you brought me." Skipping to keep up with the fast pace Summer had set, and also out of excitement, Sparrow seemed to be on the verge of becoming airborne. Talk about natural highs. Sparrow could conjure one up out of nothing and for no reason.

"Good question," Summer said. "Can't think why I'd be so stupid. Maybe I ought to send you back."

Sparrow stopped in midskip and stared in consternation, until Summer's, "Come on. I was just kidding," set her bouncing again.

Where the trail narrowed in the first grove, Summer slowed down and let Sparrow take the lead. Elbows and knees flying, braids bobbing, she romped on ahead as full of mindless joy as one of the Crown Ridge colts frolicking across the pasture. Still skipping, she crossed the clearing, passing the bloody spot beside the trail without a glance. Summer let her go.

There were things that needed to be said, instructions that had to be given, but they could wait until they'd reached the road and passed the place where she'd found Cerbe. There'd be time enough when that was behind them to make sure that Sparrow understood what would be required of her. Out on the Fishers' road at last, she called Sparrow back to walk beside her.

"Are you listening?" she asked. "I have some very important things to tell you. If you don't listen, you're going to make a lot of terrible mistakes and the Olivers will probably send you right home."

Sparrow's eyes widened and she nodded solemnly. "I'm listening," she said.

"Well, first of all, don't touch anything unless I tell you to; and when I tell you what you can do, do it as hard as you can and over and over again until I tell you to stop."

"Okay. What am I going to do? What are you going to tell me to do?"

Summer grabbed Sparrow's arm, pulled her to a stop and surveyed her critically. One side of her collar was tucked in and a loose strand of hair fell across her forehead. Summer put things right while she answered the question. "Well, I think I'll let you sweep the patio first. Do you think you could do a good job on the patio?"

Sparrow was positive that she could.

The sun was high when they reached Crown Ridge, and the trainer's van was in the driveway. That meant Nan was probably in the stable or ring. She always watched when the trainer worked with the colts. After putting Sparrow to work in the back patio, Summer went first to the stable. Nan wasn't there but Victor, the man who kept the stalls clean and groomed the horses, was working in Scimitar's stall.

"You looking for Mrs. Oliver?" he said. "She's down to the circle with the trainer."

When she reached the riding arena, Summer found Nan leaning on the fence watching the trainer work with Falcon, the beautiful gray three year old who was just learning to be a saddle horse.

"I'm sorry I'm late," Summer began, but Nan interrupted.

"Look. Josh is going to ride Falcon—for the first time." The trainer was shaking the saddle, pulling hard on the stirrup. The horse, a light dapple gray with a silvery mane and tail, looked back as if in surprise. But when the trainer slipped his foot into the stirrup and suddenly rose into the saddle, nothing much happened. The trainer spoke softly to Falcon, nudging him gently with his heels. After a moment the colt moved forward a few steps, stopped, and moved forward again. It wasn't until the trainer had dismounted that Nan turned to Summer.

"Now, what is it, dear?" she said.

"I said, I was sorry I was late. Something happened and—well, I have to take care of my little sister today, so I had to get her ready and bring her with me. I hope it's okay. I'd have asked first but—you know, no phone and everything. And I couldn't go off and leave her alone."

"Well, I suppose it will be all right." Nan

sounded doubtful. "But I hope she won't need too much supervision. You'll have to work very fast to finish as it is."

As they started back to the house, Summer explained about how much help Sparrow was going to be, and how she had already started sweeping the patio, and what a hard worker she was for a seven-year-old. But then in the stable, there she was, still clutching the broom as she hung over the gate of Greybird's stall—after she'd promised on her word of honor not to quit sweeping until Summer came back and told her she could. To make matters worse, she didn't even put out her hand and say hello, the way Summer had told her to do when she was introduced. Instead she just went on hanging over the rail babbling about the horse. Summer wanted to jerk her down to the ground and shake her, until she looked at Nan and realized what was happening. When Summer went in and started the scrubbing, Nan and Sparrow were both hanging over the rail. Nan was talking about manes and fetlocks and bays and sorrels, and Sparrow was listening with her eyes like saucers—if saucers were ever bright blue and fringed with coppery lashes.

Sometime later, while she was doing the bathrooms, she went back into the kitchen for a can of cleanser to find Sparrow at the table in the breakfast room, and Nan taking things out of the refrigerator. There were already berries and cream and scones and a big glass of milk on the table.

"Summer," Nan said. "You'd better sit right

down here with your little sister and have a bite to eat. If you're as hungry as she is, you must be—"

"No thank you," Summer interrupted in a tone of voice that made both Nan and Sparrow look at her in surprise. "I'm not hungry right now," she added quickly with a smile that was definitely window dressing. Behind it an angry resentment tightened her jaws and burned across her cheeks.

Back in the bathroom, on her knees beside the tub, she told herself she was an idiot. What had she been so angry about? Wasn't what seemed to be happening exactly what she'd planned? Or was it? Actually she hadn't planned anything for sure. What she had done, in bringing Sparrow with her to the Olivers, was more like opening a door. She'd made no decision about whether or not she was going any farther, or whether Sparrow—the resentment flooded back—or whether Sparrow, the little boot-licker, was going any farther.

Spraying Windex on the mirror a little later, she caught sight of her frowning face . . . and grinned.

Wow! What a witch! I almost scared myself. I don't really know what was eating me. To accuse Sparrow of cozying up to Nan was obviously your basic pot and kettle situation. Only worse. Because in this case the kettle—Sparrow, that is—couldn't be any more clean and shiny. She may have her problems, but being sneaky about anything is definitely not one of them. With Sparrow what you see is one hundred and one percent

92

what you get—nothing more and nothing less. So if she's hooked Nan already, she did it just by being her own dumb-little-friendly-puppy self.

She went on composing the letter in her head while she finished the basins and toilet and by the time she moved on to the master bedroom she was, if not in a good mood, at least able to be a little more objective. As she dusted the night stand, she examined the picture of Deborah carefully, evaluating the similarities—the thick braids, although obviously of the wrong color, and something about the upper half of the face. Nothing too noticeable, really. What would happen, would happen, she decided. It was much too early to worry one way or the other. Besides, since Richard B. wasn't at home, the largest hurdle was going to have to wait for another day.

The other part of the resentment, the part concerning Nan, was not so simple, or so simply dispensed with. It flared up several times, in fact, as the day went on and Nan continued to treat Sparrow like some kind of honored guest, instead of an assistant housekeeper. Every time Summer selected a chore that Sparrow could handle, like dusting the woodwork in the living room, Nan showed up to worry about such a little girl working so hard and to take Sparrow away with her—to look at the newest colt or to be shown the pictures in a huge photograph album in Richard's study. After working for the Olivers for almost two years, Summer had never been asked to look at the album.

Once, while Sparrow was out following the peacocks, in hopes of a fallen feather, Nan tried to pump Summer. "I don't believe you finished telling me about what happened this morning," she said, and when Summer looked pointedly blank, "The reason you were late and had to bring Sparrow with you? You started to tell me about it?"

"Oh that," Summer said. "There wasn't anything more to tell. My mother just found out at the last minute that she had to go someplace."

"Someplace?" Nan said.

"Yes. To see about a job—in Fort Bragg." The answer had popped easily into her mind—and came out so smoothly and convincingly she almost believed it herself. She didn't like lies and liars, but when it was necessary she did it competently—unlike Oriole. The idea amused her for a moment, until she remembered the lies Oriole was undoubtedly going to tell about Cerbe. Her dark mood returned then and stayed with her for the rest of the day. And when Nan invited Sparrow to come again next weekend, it did nothing at all to lift her spirits.

On the way home while Sparrow burbled with excitement about Crown Ridge—she'd loved it all: the animals, the house and Nan, apparently in that order—Summer thought some more about lies and liars. Before the day was over, there would be more of both. And because of Sparrow, she was going to have to be one of the liars. At first she'd considered the truth, and even planned exactly how it was to be told. She'd wait until they were home; and then, in front of Oriole, she would tell Sparrow exactly what

94

had happened to Cerbe. There was a part of her that fiercely wanted to tell that truth in that particular way.

But there was another part that watched Sparrow's happy face and, in imagination, changed it to the way it would look after the truth was told. And it was that part that finally won. Summer would join the liars. The only remaining problem was just which lies would be most useful, and how to get Oriole to limit herself to those. There would have to be a conference with Oriole before she had a chance to talk to Sparrow, which meant some kind of a ruse would be necessary.

As soon as they turned off the road, Summer lagged behind and then suddenly darted off the path. Hidden in a thick clump of rhododendron, she waited until Sparrow came back looking for her. "Summer. Summer." Sparrow's voice was plaintive. "Where'd you go? Stop hiding from me." Suddenly her voice brightened. "Are we playing a game, Summer? Are we playing hide and seek? Okay, here I come." After Sparrow had gone past, Summer made her way back to the path and then ran. When she reached the trailer, she found Oriole sitting on the front steps.

She'd planned to lie, all right. Even though her pale skin looked blotchy around her eyes and nose—a sure sign she'd been crying—she smiled when she saw Summer, a typical Oriole smile, wide-eyed and deceptively innocent.

"Hi," she said. "I found your note. I hope Sparrow didn't make a nuisance of herself."

"Listen," Summer said. "Sparrow'll be here in a

95

minute. I know what happened to Cerbe, but she doesn't."

Oriole's face disintegrated into undisguised horror before she got it under control and produced a more or less convincing portrayal of resigned grief. "It must have been a car," she said. "Angelo and I found him when—"

"No!" Summer said. "I know who killed him and where he was killed and it wasn't on the road. But I don't want Sparrow to know. Let's just say we don't know where he is. When she notices he's missing, we'll just say we don't know where he went. Okay? That way she'll get used to the idea that he's gone a little at a time."

Oriole's eyes were glassy. "She didn't see him?" she asked. "This morning?"

"No. I found him first and buried him, before she woke up."

"Oh, baby," Oriole's face crumpled, and tears filled her eyes. She held out her arms, but Summer moved away. "It wasn't Angelo's fault," Oriole said. He was just walking back to the trailer with me and Cerbe attacked him. He had to protect himself."

"With a gun? How come he was carrying a gun?"

"Summer. Why'd you run off from me?"

Sparrow was running across the clearing, and there was only time to whisper, "We don't know where he is. Okay?" before she reached the trailer.

"Hi," Sparrow said to Oriole. "Did you read our note? I got to go with Summer. And Mrs. Oliver says I can go again next Saturday, and . . ." her face

96

puckered with sudden concern. "What's the matter? What's the matter, Oriole?"

"Nothing," Oriole said. "Some dust blew in my eyes. I'd better go in and wash my face."

There was no chance to say anymore. Sparrow did all the talking during dinner, telling Oriole about her day at the ranch, babbling about the "king's palace house" and the horses and the peacocks. The peacocks had obviously made the biggest impression. It seemed that Sparrow had always thought of them as fairy tale animals like dragons and unicorns, and even though she'd seen their feathers she never really believed that they were still around in person. So seeing them at the Olivers had really blown her mind. It was almost dark before she suddenly looked around and said, "Hey, where's Cerbe?"

Oriole looked at Summer—leaving the lying to her. "Ask Oriole," she wanted to say. "Ask your mother where Cerbe is." But she didn't. Instead she said, "I don't know. Probably he's out chasing rabbits again. Why don't you go call him." Sparrow stood outside the trailer calling for a long time.

Sunday was dark and gloomy. A heavy low-flying fog resisted the sun's efforts to burn it away, and the air was damp and chill. Inside the trailer another kind of chill had to be camouflaged for Sparrow's sake, but it remained just below the surface of every contact between Summer and Oriole. Sparrow must have felt it because she was whiny and clingy, as she always was when people were fighting. And now and then when Sparrow was momentarily out of hearing,

97

the chill turned into fire and flamed out into the open. Particularly every time Sparrow went out to stand on the step and call for Cerbe.

"Well, what happens now," Summer said once while Sparrow's high-pitched wobbly call echoed and reechoed from the front steps. "Now that he's gotten rid of Cerbe is he going to move in here?"

"Oh, Summer. Don't!" Oriole said. "I don't know what's going to happen. But it wouldn't be the worst thing in the world if he did move in. You're always worrying about expenses, and all and he—"

"Oh! Does Angelo have a lot of money?"

"Well, not at the moment, but he will have before long."

A lot of Oriole's boyfriends had been just about to strike it rich—as sculptors or herb doctors or rock stars or whatever, but none of them had ever done it. And if Angelo's prospects were any better, it simply meant that Summer's worst suspicions were justified. But all she said was, "Where have I heard that before?"

At first Oriole was patient, guiltily patient, but after a while she began to get angry, and late in the afternoon she walked out. It happened while Sparrow was out looking for Cerbe for about the tenth time. They'd been arguing about Angelo again, and Summer said, "Well, all I can say is, if he moves in I'm leaving." At that point Oriole said, "No, I'm leaving." And she got her purse and left.

Summer knew she'd come back. She always did. But at three o'clock in the morning, when she finally returned, Summer was still awake—and the next day

98

was Monday, the first day of the job at Pardells'. Summer had to be in Alvarro Bay by eight o'clock.

It was a funny feeling, knocking on the door and having Pardell open it. It was like that with teachers. You knew they had lives outside of the classroom, but somehow it always gave you an odd, disoriented feeling to see them in other situations. When Pardell came to the door clutching a dishtowel and a frying pan and looking disheveled, Summer suddenly felt tongue-tied. She needn't have worried though. She didn't have to say anything. He did all the talking.

"Come in. Come in," he said, leading the way toward the kitchen. "That is, if you can get in. Meg's been gone for three days, and I've lost six pounds and two major appliances. I meant to have things straightened up a bit before I left, but I ought to be on the road in ten minutes—and look at it!"

"I've seen worse," Summer said, grinning.

"I know—but you don't remember where," Pardell said. "Look. Do what you can. I won't expect a miracle. Meg's due to be discharged from the hospital at ten-thirty so we won't be back until midafternoon. If you could just get the dishes done—and I'm afraid the service porch is going to need some attention."

He wasn't kidding about the service porch. It seemed that he'd put about three times too much detergent in the washing machine, and it had erupted like a sudsy volcano soaking several piles of dirty clothes, a stack of newspapers and the cat's bed.

Pardell disappeared then, and she attacked the service porch problem, starting a load of wash and hanging the cat's bed out to dry on the porch railing while the cat, an enormous orange tiger-stripe, watched suspiciously. She was surveying the kitchen, wondering where to begin, when Pardell struggled through on his way to the garage carrying some blankets and a wheelchair. "From Hertz-rent-a-chair," he said. "Let us put you in the driver's seat. Meg didn't want it, but the doctor insisted she use one until the cast comes off."

Summer ran to hold doors open for him while he maneuvered through the still-soggy service porch and into his old Toyota station wagon. Then she went back to face the disaster area in the kitchen.

The biggest problem was finding things. It became apparent immediately that the trouble was more deepseated than could be accounted for by Meg's three-day absence. It was obvious that Meg, herself, was no organizer. Cleaning equipment was scattered haphazardly all over the house, and the broom closet was full of music manuscripts. In spite of the fact that it wasn't a third the size of the Olivers', the Pardells' little house was at least twice as hard to clean. But, using a sysem worked out in her two years at the Olivers', Summer went at each room methodically, and by the time the Pardells pulled into the driveway some hours later, things were looking a lot better. Even Meg, pale and tired-looking and wearing a huge cast on her left leg, said she couldn't believe her eyes. And after he'd wheeled her into the bedroom, Pardell went through the house yelling, "Amazing. Incredible." and "Beyond all expectations." Summer couldn't help feeling good about it.

That was the one advantage working for the Pardells had over working for the Olivers. You worked twice as hard and got paid less, but the Pardells certainly knew how to make you feel good about it. And looking ahead at the summer that was just beginning, Summer could guess that things to feel good about were going to be in short supply.

8

I said I would leave and I haven't, so I suppose they think that sooner or later I'll start speaking to him. But I won't. He usually tries to make a joke of it, like trying to trick me into answering when he says something to me. But it's been over a month now, and I haven't said one word to him.

Oriole's finally stopped arguing with me about it. At first she kept trying to convince me that he was really a great guy, and then she gave up on that and began about what a hard life he'd had and how he'd had to be hard and tough in order to survive. She gave up on that too after a while and just quit mentioning him at all. Sometimes I think she's beginning to see what he's really like. He hasn't been here at the trailer as much lately. For a while I thought maybe he didn't actually move in because of me, but now I doubt it.

Lately I've begun to think Oriole has

been trying to keep him away from me and Sparrow, but there's more to it than that. He's still here sometimes during the day, but when it begins to get dark, he usually goes back to the Fishers'. Like there was something he had to do there after the sun goes down. Sometimes Oriole goes with him, and sometimes she doesn't.

During the week I've been taking Sparrow with me when I go to work at the Pardells'. There's a summer program at the school for kids her age, and she spends the morning there. Then she goes to play at one of her friends' houses or else comes back to the Pardells' and waits for me. Of course she goes with me every Saturday when I go to Crown Ridge. So Oriole and the Creep have the trailer to themselves during the day if they want it. But when night falls, he always seems to go back to his lair—like a vampire in reverse.

I still have this feeling that something is about to happen, although the summer's one-third over already and everything's pretty much the same. Not that I've been worrying very much about it—with the two jobs there hasn't been the time—but it's still there at the back of my mind—a feeling that there's going to be a big change. I don't know what kind of one though. Right at the present it doesn't look as if there will be any changes because of the Olivers.

Sparrow rolled over, stretched and opened her eyes, blinking at the light. "Summer! Aren't you ever going to go to sleep? The light's keeping me awake." Actually she'd been sleeping peacefully for at least an hour.

Summer smiled at her. "As a matter of fact," she said, "I was just about to stop. So quit whining." She got up to put the letter in the box, and by the time she was back Sparrow was asleep again. She didn't even wake up when Summer shoved her over to her own side of the bed. She said something but it must have been part of a dream, because it was about Marina. Summer sighed. She'd been carrying on about Marina again lately, pestering Summer to get the Fishers to let her visit.

It was a bright night, the radiance of an almost full moon turning everything—even the interior of the trailer—into scenes of eerie beauty; scenes that persisted even after Summer determinedly closed her eyes. Moonlit landscapes that shifted and mutated into first one familiar setting and then another.

The breakfast room at Crown Ridge—with Richard reading the morning paper and Nan supervising as Sparrow arranged a bouquet of gladiolas in a large ceramic vase. From where she was working at the kitchen sink, Summer could see and hear as Nan enthused over Sparrow's efforts and then invited Richard to enthuse, too—over the artistic arrangement supposedly but also, quite obviously, over Sparrow herself. It didn't work, however. Richard said yes, the flowers were nice, and went back to his paper. Whatever Nan was planning for Sparrow, and Summer felt quite certain she was planning something, it was pretty clear that Richard wasn't ready to go along with Nan's scenario. While he had stopped arguing that Sparrow ought to be left at home, on the grounds that she would interfere with Summer's work, he continued to show very little interest in Sparrow herself. And it was apparent to Summer that Nan's transparent efforts to make him feel as she did about Sparrow were doing more harm than good.

And at the Pardells'? The only change threatening there was the fact that Meg's cast was due to come off sometime in July and the job would probably be over. Six hours a day, five days a week was adding up to a lot more money than she'd ever been able to earn before. And when the job ended, the rapid growth of the bank account would end too, and that would be too bad.

Of course, the work wasn't easy. Trying to introduce some kind of order into a household consisting of Alan and Meg Pardell was turning out to be an almost superhuman task. The trouble was they were too much alike. In some ways they were both organized and efficient and competent—Alan with words and Meg with music. But where taking care of a house and car and their personal belongings were concerned they were both borderline retarded.

When a day at the Pardells' ended—a day of cleaning and shopping and finding things and putting them back in their right places and making lunch for Meg and herself and ushering in and out Meg's piano students and finding more things and putting them back in their right places, Summer would go home at three-thirty in the afternoon leaving things in fairly good order. But after Alan had made dinner and breakfast, with Meg coaching from her wheelchair, and dashed off to work . . . in the wheezy old car when it was running and on the bus when it wouldn't—Summer would return to find a shambles. A special kind of Pardellian shambles in which almost any article, including the large cat, could suddenly disappear as if into a maelstrom. And on Mondays, after two days of Pardell's housekeeping, you needed a map to find your way to the kitchen.

There were also some other aspects of life at the Pardells' for which an outsider needed a map, or if not a map at least a list of the rules of the game. Because, without instructions, you were likely to think that the Pardells were both absolutely insane, instead of just mildly crazy.

One of their games concerned their disorganized lifestyle. The game plan seemed to be that they each claimed to be the soul of efficiency and blamed all their problems on the other. Pardell blamed all his disasters in the kitchen on the haphazard system he'd inherited from Meg, and Meg claimed she was keeping track of the things he'd lost. She was always saying, "I've counted, you know. I know exactly how many household items Alan has lost during our entire marriage. It's over three thousand now. Three thousand and eighty-three, to be exact." The amount varied since she had a poor memory for numbers, but it was generally somewhere in the thousands. And when Pardell told stories about burned meals and fungus gardens in the refrigerator, Meg would mention the time when she'd left him baby-sitting and he'd misplaced the baby.

There was another game about how Meg would have been a concert pianist if she hadn't married Alan —and then Pardell would tell about how he gave up his career as a serious writer to marry Meg.

There was also an Odious game. Odious was the orange tomcat. Both Alan and Meg pretended to hate him and blame his presence in the house on each other. They each had a large repertoire of disgusting cat stories, which they often told at the very moment they were allowing Odious to climb all over them or sneak things off their plates at the table.

It took Summer a while to understand how the Pardells really felt about Odious, and about a lot of other things. Or at least to find out that they didn't really feel the way they said they did. She found the fact that she couldn't ever count on either of them meaning exactly what they said either frustrating or funny, depending on her frame of mind.

It must have been somewhere around ten o'clock when Summer's mind quit dredging up real Oliver and Pardell memories and shifted down into dreamed-up ones. She'd been very tired that night, and she must have been sleeping deeply because she was only vaguely aware of Sparrow's climbing over her. Ordinarily, Sparrow on her way to the bathroom, half-awake and clumsy, managed to knee her in the stomach, get tangled in her hair and, in general, thoroughly wake her up. But this time she barely registered Sparrow's departure. It was quite a while later that she suddenly came fully awake knowing that a

107

great deal of time had passed and Sparrow hadn't returned. And also knowing in some strange interior way that something was very wrong.

It took only a minute to confirm her sudden conviction that she was all alone in the trailer. The bathroom was empty, and so was Oriole's bedroom. She still hadn't returned from the Fishers', or wherever she went almost every night with Angelo. And where Sparrow had gone was easy to guess. She'd had that dream again and had gone looking for Marina. For several minutes Summer stood on the front steps calling—just as Sparrow still called almost every day for Cerbe—and just as uselessly. In the moon-bright forest stillness, the sound of her own voice frightened her—a long throbbing wail like the cry of a lost animal. Then she ran back to the bedroom, pulled on jeans, shoes and a jacket, grabbed her flashlight and ran down the path toward the road and the Fishers'.

On the path, beneath the branches of the tall trees, it was very dark in spite of the full moon; but when she reached the road, she switched off the flashlight and went on running. She ran for a long way—up the steep road, at times scrambling up shortcuts between the frequent switchbacks. At last sharp cramps in her legs and a searing pain in her chest forced her to stop. She dropped to her knees and crumped against the embankment. It wasn't until the pain had subsided and her ears were no longer deafened by the thunder of her heart and the rasp of her breath that she began to listen—and to think.

Just ahead the road was leveling out, which meant she was almost to the wide plateau where the Fishers lived. She listened, trying to hold her breath, but

108

there was no sound except for the faint rustle of a brisk ocean wind in the surrounding pine trees. The road ahead, which she had walked many times in the days when the McIntyres were welcome visitors, was a narrow canyon between tall trees and thick underbrush. And at the end of the road there would be—what? The dog-murdering Creep, Neanderthal Bart, slimy little Jude, dangerous watchdogs, and whatever was behind all the mysterious changes of the past months. If she got up and went on, she would walk alone and in the dark into the midst of whatever it was.

It was not something she had planned on when she dashed out of the trailer in pursuit of Sparrow. If she had thought at all, it must have been that she would catch up with Sparrow while she was still on the road. But she hadn't, and now she would have to decide what to do next. Whether to give up and go home—or to keep on going.

A sane, reasonable-sounding voice in her mind argued against it. "Go back," it said. "She probably isn't here anyway. She probably curled up and went to sleep somewhere in the trailer, the way she does, and just didn't hear you calling. Or maybe she turned off the road to go to that secret tree stump of hers and Marina's, and if you start back maybe you'll find her on her way home." But there was another part of her, the stubborn, hardheaded part that had always made her swim against the current, that answered the reasonable voice with a firm, "No." Nothing else just "No." She said it out loud—stood up—and started on up the road.

The gate was new. Fastened with a heavy chain

and padlock, it crossed the road just as it emerged from the heavily wooded hillside and entered the clearing. Moving as quietly as she could on the graveled surface, Summer crept forward until she could peer between the crossbars. At first, in the uncertain soft-edged moonlight, everything looked just as it always had. Ahead of her was the big house, an enormous log cabin with a wide stone chimney and deep veranda. A light was on in the living room, but no one was visible through the small-paned windows. Just to the right was the grape arbor and the large gazebo that Galya called the summer house, and farther back, behind the arbor, Summer could see the dim outline of the smokehouse and beyond that the small cabin that had belonged to the grandfather. The smokehouse was dark, but a light shone in the window of the old cabin.

Farther to the right were the enormous greenhouses—first the two familiar old ones and, beyond them, dimly seen in the distance, what seemed to be at least two more, where the raised beds of the summer gardens had been before. A high gate and new greenhouses, but nothing else. No sign of patroling dogs or humans. Cautiously, Summer climbed to the top of the gate, and then down the other side.

She had just reached the ground when a sudden sharp noise made her drop down and cower against the gatepost, trying vainly to compress herself into its narrow shadow. The front door of the house opened, and a long swath of golden light shot out across the yard. In the middle of that pathway of light lay an elongated human shadow. Summer raised her head and turned slowly and carefully until she was able to see the person to whom the shadow belonged. It was Oriole.

Carrying what seemed to be a large tray, Oriole crossed the veranda, descended the steps and took the path that led past the arbor toward the far side of the clearing and Dyedushka's cabin. Still crouching, Summer watched until she reached the cabin and disappeared inside. Seeing Oriole made Summer feel a little less frightened. Oriole wouldn't be calmly carrying a tray if Sparrow had been chewed up by dogs or shot by an itchy-fingered guard. There was even the possibility that the tray was for Sparrow—a bedtime snack before she was taken back to the trailer.

A split second later and Summer would have been in the midst of the yard at the very moment when the man and dog came out of the house. As it was, she had taken only a step or two when she heard the front door open again. There was time to jump back into the shadow of the gate before the huge man called Bart and an enormous doberman came down the steps and headed across the yard.

Fright was a hot hand squeezing her throat. Cowering on the ground, certain that at any moment the dog would get her scent and race toward her, she tried to make herself leap up and climb the gate. But she couldn't move—and the dog kept on going in the direction of the greenhouses, tugging eagerly at his leash. When they reached the first greenhouse, Bart opened the door, and he and the dog went inside. Summer got shakily to her feet.

This time she turned sharply to the left, keeping

111

in the shadows of the trees that edged the cleared land. She would circle around the house until she came to the far side of the clearing and the old cabin, keeping the big house between herself and the greenhouses—and keeping the wind in her face, the strong wind that had undoubtedly saved her already by blowing her scent away from the doberman. She had gone several yards, moving silently on the carpet of pine needles, when she stopped again, paralyzed by a sudden sound. A rapping noise, not loud but very near. It seemed to come from the direction of the house. Shrinking back into the deeper shadows below the trees, Summer listened and watched.

The house was not far away, but the windows in this rear wall were dark and silent. The first, Summer knew, opened on the room that had been Marina's, and the next two were in the boys' bedrooms. The rooms were dark—empty or occupied by sleepers; but the noise went on. *"Rap, rap, rap,"*—a pause, and then the same thing again. A soft persistent knocking. Gradually curiosity got the better of fear, and Summer moved forward, following the sound, until she could see that a blurred shape, which had seemed to be only a part of a large camellia bush, was actually something separate. Separate and alive and dressed in a flannel nightgown—Sparrow!

"Sparrow," Summer whispered, and the small, shadowy figure below Marina's window froze into immobility. But then, as Summer moved cautiously forward, there was a sharp gasp, a flurry of motion and Sparrow's arms were wrapped tightly around her waist.

112

"Oh, Summer. I'm so glad you're here. Marina came again and told me to come so I did, but she won't come to her window and I was so frightened."

"Shh!" Summer put her hand over Sparrow's mouth. "Keep your voice down." She unwrapped Sparrow's arms, and grasping her firmly by her wrist, she headed back for the shelter of the trees. But Sparrow resisted.

"No. No. Knock on the window first. On the glass. I couldn't reach the glass. I want to see Marina."

"Marina's in Lodi."

"No. No, she's not. She's here. I know she's here." Sparrow's voice was getting louder again, and she struggled fiercely, digging in her heels and trying to wrench her wrist out of Summer's grasp. Her voice had taken on the high-pitched wail that usually preceded a fit of hysterical crying. In frightened desperation, Summer capitulated.

"Okay. Okay," she whispered. "We'll look. We'll look to see if Marina's in her room. Now please, be still. Okay."

Sparrow gulped and nodded. Clutching Summer's hand, she pulled her back toward Marina's window. Summer held back, moving slowly while she wondered desperately what she was going to do. Knocking on the glass was out. With Marina away, someone else was probably using her room, possibly one of Angelo's thugs. But somehow Sparrow had to be convinced.

Standing below the window, the solution came to her. "I'll look," she said. She probably couldn't see anything at all in the dark room, but she'd pretend to, and possibly Sparrow would be satisfied. She put one foot in the crevice between two logs, grasped the window sill and pulled herself up until her face was level with the pane.

But she did see something. A dim light was coming from down low near the floor—a night light. Marina had always been afraid to sleep in a dark room. Summer's eyes moved to the left, to where Marina's bed was barely discernible: a white spread folded at the foot, a dark blanket and a small, dark head on the pillow. Summer was still staring in startled disbelief when the window in the next room went up with a noisy bang. Sparrow shrieked; and not far away, the dog began to bark.

"Ssst," a voice whispered. "Come here. Quick." Summer looked up from where she crouched, clutching Sparrow, between the cabin's foundation and the camellia bush. The upper half of a body was protruding from the next window, the arms motioning wildly. "Summer. Come here." It wasn't until he said her name that she recognized the voice as Nicky's.

She didn't stop to argue. Pulling Sparrow to her feet, she dragged her toward Nicky's window by the back of her nightgown. "Sparrow's here, too," she whispered.

"Oh my, God," Nicky said. "Lift her up here. Hurry."

Summer hurried, and Sparrow, who had been flailing around wildly in terror, making herself as hard to hang onto as a flopping fish, finally realized what was happening and held up her arms. As soon as she disappeared inside the room, Nicky was back in the window. Taking his hands, Summer climbed the log wall like a ladder.

A moment later the dog was under the window, barking frantically. The narrow beam of a flashlight slashed across the room, and a loud voice growled, "Hey kid. What's going on in there."

"Get down against the wall," Nicky whispered before he leaned out the window. "Shut up," he yelled. "Shut him up." There was a harsh command, a yelp, and the dog was quiet.

"It's raccoons again," Nicky said.

"Raccoons? Where?"

"Right down there. I threw some apple cores out the window, and a few minutes ago a couple of raccoons were right down there fighting over them—until old Adolph got all excited. I thought you said you trained him not to bark at raccoons anymore."

It worked. There were some muttered words, the rattle of a jerked leash, another yelp, and everything was quiet. Summer, who'd been lying face down against the wall, pushed herself to a sitting position in time to see Nicky getting into his jeans. Then he came back and sat down crosslegged on the floor. "Well, well," he said. "You two taking up narcing?"

9

"Nicky. What on earth's going—" Summer said, before Nicky stopped her with an urgent "Shhh!" He got quickly to his feet and tiptoed to the door. His ear to the crack, he listened for several seconds and then came back. As he crouched down beside her, the bright moonlight from the open window fell directly on his face, and suddenly she realized that he wasn't nearly as calm as he'd sounded. Either his cool-sounding crack about narcing had been pure bluff, or else the reaction hadn't set in until the crisis was past and Bart and the dog had gone. But now fear glittered in his eyes and twitched at his mouth.

"Listen," he whispered so softly she could scarcely hear. "We've got to get you out of here right away. As soon as Bart finishes his patrol. We'll have to hurry." When Sparrow started to whisper something about Marina, he reached over and put his hand across her mouth. "No," he said firmly. "Be still." And she was.

He went back then and listened at the door for

what seemed a very long time. From where she was crouching under the window with Sparrow huddled against her, Summer could hear the sound of distant voices, footsteps and finally the heavy slam of a door. She waited, holding back her own fear by concentrating on Sparrow, who was shivering violently and now and then sobbing softly under her breath. At last Nicky left the door and moved silently across the room. He picked up a jacket and was shrugging into it when he suddenly stopped, took it off and put it on Sparrow. Then he opened the window very slowly and quietly. It wasn't until he was sitting on the sill that he whispered, "Now. Let's go. Hand Sparrow down to me."

Warning her again to be quiet, Summer boosted Sparrow into the window and then down to Nicky's waiting arms. Then she climbed down herself. Nicky was moving away, motioning for them to follow. He led the way toward the trees, and she hurried after him, dragging a stumbling, sobbing Sparrow, her ears so full of the memory of the dog's roaring bark that several times she startled, momentarily convinced that it had begun again.

At the edge of the clearing, Nicky turned to the right, away from the gate. Summer hesitated, wondering what he thought he was doing, until she remembered the spring path. A narrow passageway hacked out of the dense undergrowth, it led first to an artesian spring and then, after many windings, finally connected farther down the hill with the Fisher road. It was one way home, but a much longer, more roundabout way. She caught up with Nicky and grabbed his arm.

"Why can't we go by the road?" she asked.

"The dog. He'll be outside now. Tied near the summerhouse. They always leave him there after the last patrol. He'd hear you climb the gate."

It was reason enough. Summer followed without further argument. A few yards down the narrow pathway, Nicky stopped and asked for the flashlight. Shining the light on the ground ahead of him, he went forward very carefully, a step at a time. "There it is," he said. "See the wire? Don't touch it. It sets off an alarm." A thin wire, almost invisible in the darkness, stretched across the path, an inch or two off the ground.

When Sparrow and Summer had safely crossed the wire, Nicky handed Summer the flashlight and said, "I'm going back now. You'll be all right from here."

"Nicky." Summer was feeling a lot less frightened now and a lot more curious. She shone the light right in his face and said, "I want to know what's going on. It's pot, isn't it?"

Nicky looked warningly at Sparrow. "No. That is . . . I'll tell you tomorrow."

"I'm working tomorrow."

"At Pardell's?"

"Yes. At Pardell's."

After a moment's hesitation Nicky seemed to come to a decision. "I'll see you tomorrow," he said and disappeared back down the trail.

It was at least an hour later that Summer and an

exhausted, whimpering Sparrow climbed into bed. Only about five hours afterwards, they got up and left for Alvarro Bay. Sometime during those five hours Oriole had come home and gone to bed. Summer didn't expect that she would get up to see them off—and she didn't. So there was plenty of time on the trip into Alvarro Bay to impress Sparrow with the necessity of keeping quiet about what had happened. She did a thorough job of it, making sure that the list of people Sparrow was not to tell included everyone she might possibly meet in the course of the day—with Sparrow one had to be explicit. In front of the school she issued a final warning that left Sparrow wide-eyed and sober and then went on to the Pardells'. The rest of the morning was routine until, just before twelve noon, when Nicky showed up at the Pardells' front door.

Summer was startled. For a lot of reasons, she hadn't thought he would keep his word. And it had never occurred to her that he might show up at the Pardells'.

"Hi," he said. "Want to go down to The Pelican for a sandwich?"

Summer looked toward the living room where Meg was conducting her last lesson before lunch. "I have to finish fixing Mrs. Pardell's lunch, and then —" She stopped. If she hadn't needed to know so badly, she might have said no, simply from long established habit. "Okay," she said, instead. "Wait just a minute."

It was past twelve when she finished putting Meg's lunch on the table. In the living room the

119

same phrase of mutilated melody was being repeated for the umpteenth time. Summer eased into the room to a spot just inside Meg's range of vision.

"Yes?" She looked surprised. The passage of time always surprised Meg, particularly when she was teaching or playing. "Time's up, already? Thank you, Summer. I guess that's it 'til next week, Bobby." Bobby, about ten years old and a not particularly enthusiastic musician, promptly disappeared. Meg listened to a brief explanation about an invitation to lunch at The Pelican, approved thoroughly, and a few minutes later Summer was walking down Mill Street with Nicky.

It was a typical summer day. The village was crawling with typical tourists. But there was nothing typical about Nicky's behavior. Walking quickly with his hands stuffed into his pockets, he kept his eyes firmly on the ground, and for several minutes said nothing at all.

"Marina's at home, isn't she," Summer said finally.

Nicky looked up frowning. "Did you tell Sparrow?" When she shook her head, he sighed with relief. "She'd give it away for sure."

"I know."

"Look. It will be hard to talk at The Pelican. I'll get some sandwiches and meet you down by the old pier. Okay." It was the kind of suggestion that Nicky had made and Summer had turned down dozens of times in the last couple of years; but this time his motives appeared to be different. And a little later, when he led the way to a secluded spot behind a sand dune, Summer followed. Although she could only guess at what he was going to say, she was quite certain that this time when he said he wanted to talk, talk was what he had in mind.

But what Nicky had to say didn't come easily. Sitting crosslegged in the sand behind the sloping dune at the foot of the bluff, Summer nibbled on her egg salad sandwich, waiting for him to begin. For a long time he simply sat, hunched over, staring down at his sandwich, not talking or eating—or making any attempt to fool around. Nicky—whose various appetites were usually so up front. Once or twice he looked up briefly and shrugged with an unhappy smile that reminded Summer of the time, years before, when somebody stole his first bicycle. She reached out suddenly and squeezed his hand. His smile wobbled, he squeezed back and started talking.

"You've got to swear you won't tell anybody."

"Okay. I swear."

He sighed, shook his head and began. "We're in a lot of trouble."

Summer was puzzled. Growing pot in large quantities had gotten lots of people in the county in trouble in the last few years; but the kind of trouble she'd heard about had mostly been fines and confiscation of the crop, with now and then a trial that ended in probations and deferred sentences. Some renters had been put off the land, but apart from some violent encounters between growers and would-be thieves, she hadn't heard of anything very serious happening to landowners like the Fishers. "Because of the pot?" she asked.

121

"Well, yes. Because of the pot. But the real trouble is . . . See the way it happened was Jude told these dealers—I mean real professionals. At least to hear Bart tell it, Angelo's been in on smuggling runs from Central America and big deals from eastern suppliers and drug wars and assassinations—the whole bit. Anyway, Jude met them, and they were talking about wanting to get in on the Mendocino action; and then the little nerd told them about our place and the greenhouses. They decided it would be a great place to grow a crop—you know, because the narc planes wouldn't be able to spot it. Nobody would suspect anything because everyone knows about Mom's winter berries and everything."

"But Galya always said she'd never get involved with growing pot."

"Yeah, I know. At first she and Dad both said no. But these guys kept on talking about how easy it would be and how much money we'd all make, and after a while they gave in. Then they all moved in, Jude and Angelo and the hulk."

"Bart?"

"Yeah, him. The first thing they did was to make my folks take Marina out of school. They said it was just because she couldn't be trusted to keep her mouth shut about what was going on; but pretty soon it was more like they were holding her hostage. And after my dad tried to back out on the whole deal, they began to keep Marina shut up in the house all the time with one of them watching her. They made my dad build that new gate, and recently they've strung tripper wires on all the paths around the clearing,

122

like that one on the way to the spring. Every time my dad starts to object to anything, Angelo starts making threats—about how an accident could happen to Marina if the rest of us don't cooperate."

"My God," Summer said.

"Yeah. I know."

"Couldn't you just go to the sheriff?"

"Dad's afraid to. He says Angelo keeps telling him about how innocent people can get shot by accident in a raid, and how, if our place is raided, he has a feeling that it will be the innocent who will suffer. God, Summer. Jerry's scared to death. You know how crazy he is about Marina. He's absolutely paralyzed. All he can think about now is getting the crop harvested and getting rid of those terrorists without any of the family getting hurt. I've tried to talk him into letting me tell the narcs, but he won't listen. I think if we knew just exactly when the raid was going to be, we could all hide or something just before and . . ."

Nicky was still talking, but Summer had lost track of exactly what he was saying. Her mind had gone blank, and a dark whirlpool of corrosive anxiety was beginning to spin in her stomach. She closed her eyes, fighting an almost overpowering urge to jump up and run.

"Summer?" Nicky was looking at her apprehensively. "What is it? What's the matter?"

She shook her head, unable to speak, fighting the need to run until she found Oriole.

"Yeah," Nicky said suddenly. He reached out toward her; and then, as if not knowing what kind

123

of contact he wanted to make, he left his hand in midair. "Look. It's not her fault. You know how she is about good-looking guys. And she doesn't really know what's going on. My mom hasn't told her about the threats and everything. All she knows is what he's told her, and he can be Mr. Nice-Guy when he wants to be. He had all of us fooled at first. Even Jerry, and you know how suspicious he is. Oh, she knows about the crop, of course, she helped plant it; but she just doesn't have any idea about the rest of it. Come on, Summer. Snap out of it."

She breathed deeply, letting in the fierce anger that could burn the panic away. "There are some things she knows." The words sounded bitten. "She knows that he shot Cerbe."

Nicky's dark eyes narrowed, and something happened to his jawline. He slammed his fist down on his leg, tipping his sandwich into the sand. He stared at it for a moment, and then he picked it up and threw it a long way down the beach: two whole wheat flying saucers trailing a comet's tail of roast beef particles. A startled sea gull skittered away, cocked its head and followed the trail, gulping greedily. Summer giggled hysterically, and Nicky put both arms around her. She stiffened, waiting for the next move, but it didn't come.

"Damn him! Damn him to hell!" Nicky's voice grated with bitter, frustrated anger; and almost of their own volition, Summer's arms went around him. She shivered, and the shiver turned into a continuing inner commotion that she couldn't quite identify. There was her own fear and anger, and Nicky's, and the relief of sharing all of it. And the shock of finding that the relief was almost as fierce as the anger. At last Nicky sighed sharply and turned her loose so suddenly she almost fell over. Grabbing her by the shoulders, he shook her hard, frowning angrily.

"What am I going to do?" he demanded; but when she opened her mouth to answer, he shook her again and said, "Don't tell me. I've got to decide myself. I've got to—" He let go of her shoulders and looked at his watch. "We'd better get back to The Pelican" he said urgently and jumped to his feet.

"Why?" Summer said.

"The nerd is picking me up there." He looked at his watch. "In about fifteen minutes."

"Did he bring you in to town?" Summer said in amazement.

"Yeah. He thinks people might start getting suspicious if Adam and I quit coming to town. So when he has to go someplace, he usually leaves one of us off here. We're supposed to see our friends—act normal—talk to people to find out if anyone suspects. He tells us what we're to talk about and what we're not to talk about, every time he brings us in."

They were halfway up the steep path that led up the bluff when Nicky suddenly pulled her to a stop. "Look, Summer. Remember you promised not to tell anyone. Not anyone. Particularly not Oriole. Even if she didn't tell him, she couldn't help acting different if she knew about the threats and everything. And he'd get it out of her. If he found out that she knew, he'd be sure that you did, too. So promise again —that you won't say a word to anyone."

125

"But what are you going to do?"

"I don't know yet. Nothing maybe. But if I do decide to do anything I'll let you know first."

"Promise."

"Well—okay. I promise."

During the rest of the day, she refused to think about it. Instead she just kept very busy, a technique that, when successful, made it possible to at least postpone the panic. It was still there, the dark, mind-swallowing wave of anxiety, lurking behind the mental barricades, but for the moment at least it was not in control. And this time Meg was there to help—Meg and women's lib and hand guns.

Meg was always into various political movements —Summer could remember seeing her manning a variety of sign-up tables—and two of her current favorites were women and guns. She was pro women and con guns. It just happened that her piano students for that afternoon were away on vacation and she was at loose ends and in the mood for conversation. So while Summer was working at the sink, Meg wheeled herself and her mending basket into the kitchen and began a debate. Summer took the opposite points of view, not through conviction, but because she was good at taking the opposite point of view and also just to keep Meg going. With Meg holding forth on women and guns, there was no time to think about Oriole.

Oriole was at home when Summer and Sparrow got there that afternoon, but so was he—lounging on the foam rubber like a Roman emperor. The clothing wasn't Roman—urban cowboy boots and a Euro-

pean-cut shirt open halfway down his hairy chest—
but the smile was. The smile was Nero or Caligula.

"Hullo, ladies," he said. And, as Summer headed
for her room, "Well then, hullo, Sparrow, and good-
by, Dummy." Lately "Dummy," with a hard nasty
edge to it, had taken the place of phony amusement
and "Garbo" or "Gabby." She liked Dummy better.
At least it was out front.

Through the thin wood of the sliding door, Summer listened carefully to the conversation that followed—the Creep finishing a story he'd apparently
been telling Oriole, something about a winning streak
he'd had once in Las Vegas. And then Oriole ques-
tioning Sparrow about her day at summer school.
Sparrow was comparatively untalkative. Afraid,
probably, to say much for fear of saying something
she shouldn't. Poor kid. Summer had not only lied to
her—about what she had seen when she looked in
Marina's window—but also had scared her to death
with terrible stories about what would happen if she
told about the midnight visit to the Fishers'. The
strain of her effort to keep her tongue under control
must have been obvious. "What's the matter, baby?"
Summer heard Oriole say. "Are you tired?"

"Yes, I'm tired. I'm very tired," Sparrow said
quickly in what was clearly a "that's-a-good-idea"
tone of voice. "I think I'll go rest. I'm going to go
in the bedroom and rest."

The door slid open, and Sparrow came in looking
pleased with herself. "I didn't tell," she whispered.
"Did you hear how I didn't tell?"

Summer stayed in her room until she heard the

127

Creep leave. She had to come out then and pretend that she didn't know that Oriole's latest lover was not only a pot grower and drug dealer, which Oriole obviously knew, but also a blackmailer and terrorist, which perhaps she didn't know. Trying to behave normally, Summer answered when spoken to and even volunteered a few comments, all the while watching Oriole and wondering.

Most of the evening she was very prudent, but at one point she couldn't resist asking, "How are the Fishers?" Oriole's phony answer, a crassly cheerful lie, brought justifying anger, so she went on to ask, "What do they hear from Marina? Will she be coming home soon?"

She threw the questions out like a baited hook, staring at Oriole, a surface smile hiding a bitter "this-ought-to-be-good" expectancy. But this time Oriole couldn't rise to the bait. She lifted her eyes slowly to Summer's. The phony cheerfulness was gone, and in its place was something so helpless and pathetic that the hard satisfying anger disappeared and in its place was, once again, the threatening shadow of the dark wave.

10

Crown Ridge was glorious that morning. The breeze smelled of sunlit forest and distant ocean, and the wide stretch of lawn, bordered by flower beds and sprinkled with peacocks, was like a commercial photo, too rich in color to be believed. Sparrow squealed with delight and ran. Summer followed more slowly.

Sparrow was still fascinated by the peacocks. She'd given them all names—Princess Topknot, Prince Rainbow, Royal Mightiness—and made up stories about them. Fantasy-type stories about kings and queens and fairy godmothers, obvious spins-offs from her favorite fairy tales. She was so intrigued by the luxurious beauty of their feathered exteriors, she seemed never to have noticed their less enchanting qualities, such as their loud, raucous voices and their aloof, antisocial behavior. Slowing to a walk and then to a crawl, she managed to get quite near the panic-prone flock before she came to a stop. She was squatting, chattering away at the big dumb birds, as Summer appoached.

"Hello, your Royal Mightiness. Have you had your breakfast yet? I'll ask Nan to let me feed you. Would you like that? Would you like me to bring you some nice breakfast?"

The peacocks went on stalking across the lawn, their heads nodding to some weird reptilian rhythm, while Sparrow watched them, and Summer watched her. Her eyes wide and glowing, her mouth partly open, Sparrow was as completely out of the real world as if she were stoned. Miles away, floating somewhere in a dream of palaces and peacocks and princesses, she was entirely unaware that Summer had caught up and was staring at her. Living completely in and for the moment—that was Sparrow for you. A Chicken Little who would never notice that the sky was falling until it hit her, not if the sun was shining however briefly and there was something fun to do or pretty to look at. Just like Oriole. Just like Oriole in a lot of ways, including her looks —the fragile-faced, pliable prettiness that attracted everybody, especially the ones who were looking for easy prey.

"Come on, Sparrow," Summer said. "We've got things to do."

There was a great deal to do that morning, more even than usual, since Richard was due to arrive home shortly before noon with some special guests who were going to stay for lunch. The guests were business associates, Nan said, some of the new partners who were involved in the expansion and who had come out from New York to look at the California plant.

Elmira, the extra help who came whenever there was a party, arrived soon after Summer and Sparrow and set to work in the kitchen, while Nan made flower arrangements and set the table in the dining room. When the cleaning was done, Summer was to help in the kitchen and do part of the serving, since Elmira would be very busy with the souffles.

Richard and his guests arrived around twelve-thirty in two cars, Richard's solemn blue Cadillac and a suavely silver Mercedes Benz. Summer and Sparrow watched from the kitchen window as five businesslike men and one even more businesslike woman got out of the car and Nan, cool and classy in a cotton lace dress, went out to meet them. A bar had been set up on the patio, and there were to be drinks there before everyone came in to lunch. As soon as they were all drinking, Summer in a white cap and apron, was to take out the tray of hot hors d'oeuvres.

She didn't plan it ahead of time at all. It came to her suddenly while she was arranging the parsley around the edge of the tray—and Sparrow was still standing on tiptoe at the window with the sunlight making a coppery halo around her head. Picking up a paring knife, Summer sliced the stems off some bunches of parsley and then carefully ran the sharp blade over the end of her forefinger.

"Damn," she said. "I've cut myself."

Hot hors d'oeuvres can't wait, the closest bandages were in the master bathroom, and Elmira was

131

too busy with the souffles to put up much of an argument. A few moments later after a quick rehearsal, Sparrow, with the frilly apron tied around her tiny waist over well-worn jeans, was off to the patio with the hors d'oeuvres tray. On her way to the bathroom, with a paper towel around her bleeding finger, Summer paused by the French doors long enough to hear Sparrow's clear little voice giving a Sparrowish version of what Summer had told her to say. "Summer cut herself with the parsley so I had to bring the horders"—and the chorus of ooohs and aaahs and questions and comments that followed.

It could have all gone wrong. Nan and Richard could have been angry. But they weren't, or if they were, they forgot about it later because of the way things turned out. Summer stayed in the bathroom for a long time, and Nan and Sparrow had to do the serving. Apparently Sparrow was the hit of the party. Everyone made a big fuss over her, and when it was all over, Richard actually picked her up and carried her out to the driveway to say good-by. That afternoon when Sparrow gave Nan her usual good-by hug, Richard asked for one, too. And for once Nan had sense enough not to comment.

It was beginning to look as if a door that had refused to budge, in spite of Nan's obvious pushing, had started to come ajar. Not a magical door that led to some wonderful daydream castle, but one that just might lead to a last resort umbrella for Chicken Little in case the sky fell before the summer was over.

On Monday, Summer began what was to be her last week of work for the Pardells'. Meg's cast had

132

been removed, and after a few days of getting used to her crutches, she'd be able to take over. At least, that was what she said. Alan didn't agree. He wanted Summer to stay on for at least another two or three weeks. "Look," he said to Meg while they were all having tea and Summer's homemade oatmeal cookies on Monday afternoon, "if those crutches bring down your domestic efficiency rating by even a degree, we may get posted by the department of health."

Meg laughed and said that he'd have to go back to getting along without oatmeal cookies and ironed handkerchiefs sooner or later, and the state of their checkbook suggested that sooner was a good idea. And Alan said, "Do you mean to tell me that you've found it?" And Summer asked, "Found what?" and Meg said, "Our checkbook. It's been missing since Saturday. Since right after someone-who-shall-re-main-nameless used it to pay the paper boy." Alan was pleading guilty and throwing himself on the mercy of the court when Summer got up and got a checkbook off the sinkboard.

"Impossible," Alan said. "I looked in that very same spot at least a dozen times last night."

"Well," Summer said, "that was before I found it under the cushion of your favorite chair—just this morning."

So Alan said, "See, we can't do without her." And Meg said maybe he was right and she'd think about it and check it out with the checkbook, now that it had reappeared.

Summer hoped, hoped very much—hoped desperately in fact—that Meg would decide to continue

133

the job. It wasn't just the money. Important as it was, the money was a small part of it. A larger factor was having someplace to go every day to get away from the trailer and Oriole and the Creep. But there was another reason that was more difficult to define, something uncertain and nebulous, but that had to do with a feeling of restfulness. A feeling that she had at the Pardells' and nowhere else. It made no sense because she worked longer and harder at the Pardells' than at the Olivers', and she often went home feeling exhausted—physically exhausted, at least. But while she was scrubbing the cracked linoleum in Meg's kitchen or chatting with Alan over tea and cookies at the end of the day, something else rested. Something deep in the pit of her stomach and crammed into the dark corners of her mind rested at the Pardells' in a way that it never really did anywhere else.

On Tuesday, Meg, who was beginning to get around quite well on crutches, went into Fort Bragg with Alan. While he taught, she would spend the day at the library and visiting friends. Summer was to have a half day off. In the morning she would do a little cleaning and keep an eye on Linda and Patrick Boyles who were coming to practice on Meg's piano, since eight-year-old Patrick was the type one did not leave alone with a defenseless piano. After that, she was free to go. Since arriving home early was out of the question, she had promised Sparrow an afternoon at the beach.

At noon, after the practice had been supervised and Patrick bandaged following an ill-advised attempt to tease Odious, Summer was making sandwiches for herself and Sparrow when the doorbell rang. Sparrow, who got out of summer school at twelve o'clock, had apparently made it across town in record time. Summer called for her to come in and went on spreading mustard. When she looked up a moment later, Nicky was standing in the kitchen door.

When she first saw him, standing there looking uncertain, an entirely unexpected feeling made her begin to smile, before her well-trained sense of self-preservation sounded the alarm. How did he find out she was going to be alone in the house? She turned the smile into a threatening scowl.

Nicky looked at the knife in her hand and began to grin. "Don't," he said, "I'd die of mustard poisoning."

The scowl and smile collided and produced something that wasn't either one. "What are you doing here?" she asked.

Nicky's grin suddenly disappeared, and he looked around cautiously. "I just wanted to talk to you." With the smile gone, his face looked suddenly tense and drawn and strangely older. "I've got to talk to somebody," he said. His shrug was somehow a gesture of despair. "It's such a hopeless mess, and I can't decide what to do. But if I don't do something, I think something terrible is about to happen."

Alarmed, Summer said quickly. "Why? What are you thinking about doing?"

"Shh," Nicky said looking towards the living room. "Where are they? The Pardells?"

135

So he hadn't known she was alone! She told him then about the Pardells being away and what her plans were for the afternoon. And by the time Sparrow arrived, she'd finished making a third salami and cheese sandwich. Then she put Odious out, locked up the house, and the three of them started out for the beach.

Sparrow did most of the talking on the way to the beach. She had seemed to accept Summer's explanations, that night at the Fishers', but now with a new source of information it became obvious that her curiosity hadn't been completely satisfied. Hanging on to Nicky's hand—Nicky had always been a favorite of Sparrow's—she skipped and trotted and asked questions.

"How come Jerry lets that man with the mean dog stay at your house?" she asked.

"I told you," Summer interrupted before Nicky could contradict her story, "I told you, Jerry is on another bummer and he doesn't want people visiting, so he got Bart and the dog to scare them off." Even though Jerry Fisher certainly had had occasional attacks of social deficiency, it wasn't the greatest explanation, but she'd thought it might wash with someone as naturally gullible as Sparrow. Apparently, though, it was too much for even Sparrow to swallow. She looked at Summer, not so much suspiciously as doubtfully, as if she thought Summer didn't know what she was talking about. Then she looked up at Nicky and repeated the question.

Nicky gave Summer a microscopic twitch of a grin. "Well," he said, "have you heard about the raspberry mob?" Sparrow shook her head, her eyes wide. "You probably heard Galya talking about how expensive raspberries are lately? Well, that's the whole problem. There's this rip-off gang who fence hot raspberries, and they've already tried to steal ours. So we just had to take precautions, that's all. Only Adolph, that's the new dog's name, isn't smart enough to tell our friends from raspberry pushers, so we just have to keep everybody away until the raspberry season is over."

The rest of Nicky's explanation was even more ridiculous, but Sparrow obviously liked it. Summer wasn't sure whether she actually found it believable or just entertaining; but whichever it was, she seemed to be satisfied.

They ate their lunch in the same hollow behind the sand dune where they'd sat before, while a familiar-looking sea gull watched expectantly from the top of a neighboring dune. Waiting, no doubt, for another flying sandwich. And after they'd finished eating, Sparrow fell for another of Nicky's tall tales. This one went that he had a friend who was in the market for seashells—any seashells—five cents apiece.

"We'll wait right here," he said, "until you get back. Hope you find a lot of them." So Sparrow rushed off to hunt for seashells, and Summer found to her surprise that she wasn't sorry to see her go. It was partly, of course, that she needed to know what was on Nicky's mind and what he might be thinking of doing about Angelo and company; but there was something more to it than that. There were some other things that she needed to know. After years of thinking she knew all she ever wanted to know about Nicky Fisher, she had recently begun to think that there might be some aspects of his personality she might possibly have overlooked.

On the other hand, maybe she hadn't. As soon as Sparrow was out of sight, he leaned over and tried to kiss her. She leaned away, glaring at him.

"Okay," he said. "Just checking. I thought maybe we were friends." His grin was rueful, plaintive.

She smiled back, only slightly sarcastically. "Friend is one thing," she said. "Sexual therapist is something else."

He chuckled. "McIntyre ninety-nine, Fisher zero. End of competition, okay?" He looked at her intently, without smiling. "On the level—I do need to talk to you."

He talked fast then, in between the times that Sparrow showed up to dump sandy fistfuls of shells in their laps and at their feet. The situation, it seemed, was becoming more and more tense and dangerous. Marina had gotten out and gone off to play in the forest a few times, and Angelo had found out about it and gotten very nervous. Now she was no longer being allowed out of the house, not even to play in the yard.

"One of them, either Angelo or the ape man or Jude, is always in the house," he said.

"Jude, too? I thought Jude was your friend, or at least Galya's friend. He'd probably be dead by now if it weren't for her."

"I know. Jude knows it too, the chicken-hearted

138

scum. But he's so terrified of Angelo that his knees knock together if he even looks at him. Besides he's hooked again, and Angelo keeps the stuff and won't let him have any if he doesn't play ball. When he needs a fix, he'd strangle his own grandmother if Angelo told him to."

"Do they all sleep in your house?" Summer asked.

"Bart and Jude do, on the living room couches. Angelo sleeps in Dyedushka's cabin. But he's in the house a lot, too. Barges in whenever he wants to, night or day."

Summer turned away, trying to hide what was going through her mind, burning behind her eyes. Oriole had been on her way to the old cabin that night, when Summer saw her from the gate. On her way to the cabin and Angelo. If the narcs came at night, that's where she would be, with Angelo and his guns. As if he were reading her mind, Nicky reached out and took her hand. They were both quiet. Sparrow came, and they both made appropriate comments while she deposited shells; and when she was gone again, they were still silent.

At last Nicky said. "I'm worried about Adam." Nicky had always had a thing about Adam, admiration and envy and jealousy, all mixed up together—a typical little brother–big brother thing, aggravated by the fact that Adam was good at everything that was important to adults.

"What about Adam?" she asked.

"He blames himself for what's happening, and he's determined to be the one to get us out of it. He was all for the pot thing at first, because of the money.

139

You know how Adam is about money. So now he's got this idea that it's up to him to get rid of those creeps. And I'm afraid he's going to get us all killed."

"He's not going to tell the police, is he?" Summer asked.

"No, I don't think he's planning to do that. But he might lose his temper and do something dumb. He's been on the verge several times already. And he wouldn't stand a chance. Angelo almost always has a gun on him, and that other nerd could crush Adam like a fly. He'd do it too, and love it. I think he's just hoping Adam will start something."

Nicky's face, usually so eager and open, looked tight and drawn. Summer found herself wanting to pat him, the way she did Sparrow when she hurt herself, or at least to say something comforting, only there was nothing to say.

"I'm going to do something, soon," Nicky went on, "even if it is dangerous."

"Like what?" Summer asked quickly.

"Like calling the sheriff's office. It couldn't be much more dangerous than it is already, the way things are going."

The dark fear began to seep out from its hiding places. "But what if they come when Oriole's there?" she wanted to cry, but instead she forced the fear back and asked in a voice that sounded only a little strange, "If you told the sheriff, do you think they'd come when you told them to? So you could all hide somewhere just before they come?"

"I don't know." He looked at Summer intently, and then nodded as if in sudden understanding. "I

wouldn't dare tell Oriole ahead of time. She might—
I'm afraid she'd tell him."

"No. No. She wouldn't. I think she knows now,
what he is. She didn't at first, but I think she does
now. I know Oriole, and I can tell. I think she's
afraid of him now. I think she's afraid to tell him she
doesn't want to see him anymore."

Nicky shook his head. "It wouldn't matter a lot
if she told him because she's crazy about him or
because she's afraid of him. We could all get just as
dead, either way."

"Tell me then," Summer said. "Tell me when the
raid's going to be."

Nicky put his hands on Summer's shoulders. "I
don't know if I'm going to tell the narcs. I don't know.
I'll just do what I have to; and if I can, I'll tell you
first."

Still tangled in her fear, she stared into his face
without seeing it, until he bent forward and kissed
her. The kiss felt warm and comforting and asked
nothing. She didn't pull away until she heard Sparrow scrambling up the other side of the dune.

11

There was one advantage to knowing that Oriole probably wouldn't be home. Somehow being almost certain she wouldn't be, even though that included knowing she was with Angelo, seemed in some ways easier to handle. As if it had been the not knowing that had mattered, all those years. As if vague undefined uncertainties were harder to face than real dangers, as long as the dangers were understood and expected. It made no sense, but now, when it was pretty certain that Oriole was at the Fishers' with the Creep and definitely in several kinds of danger, Summer didn't run down the path to burst into the trailer, breathless and shaking. Instead she deliberately slowed her pace, letting Sparrow skip on ahead.

Sparrow skipped across the clearing, stopped to pick up something and clattered up the steps to the trailer's door. As Summer reached the bottom stair, she heard Sparrow say, "Hi, Oriole. Look at the pretty rock I found." Oriole was at home after all. At home and alone.

She was sewing. Sitting crosslegged on the foam rubber, she was embroidering the yoke of a dress she was making for Sparrow. She was wearing a peasant blouse and a long gathered skirt. Her red gold hair made a spun sugar cloud around her face. Straight backed and slender, with her bare feet peeking out from under the ruffled skirt, she looked not much bigger than Sparrow; and if it weren't for the dark circles under her eyes, not a whole lot older. Putting the sewing aside, she held out her arms, and Sparrow threw herself into them. Summer went into the kitchen, ignoring the arm that Oriole held out to her as she passed. By the time she'd gotten herself a drink of water, they'd stopped cuddling and Sparrow had begun her usual long-playing account of the day's events. Summer sipped her water and listened.

As Sparrow babbled on about a quarrel she'd had with some kid named Conrad, and how her painting had been chosen for a place of honor on the bulletin board in the school office, Oriole listened intently, making comments like "Really?" and "Hurrah for Sparrow" and "That's beautiful, baby. That's really beautiful."

You could usually count on Oriole to be a good listener. What you couldn't count on, had never been able to count on, was her doing anything about anything you told her, no matter how important—at least not if it took any organization or effort or courage. But there was no denying that she was a good listener. She was obviously taking in every word Sparrow said —right up to the time when she got to the part about going to the beach with Nicky. That was when Sparrow began to lose Oriole's undivided attention.

"And look—" Sparrow dug into her pocket and brought out a handful of sandy nickels and dimes. "I found a whole lot of seashells, and Nicky paid me all this money. How much money is that, Oriole? It's lots, isn't it? Is it enough to go to Disneyland?" Sparrow had been saving money for a trip to Disneyland for years, except that every time she got a few dollars saved up, she always spent it on something else.

But Oriole was looking at Summer. Looking at Summer and letting her pale face tighten into a worried question that was almost as easy to interpret as if she'd asked it in one syllable words. "How much do you know?" it asked. "What did he tell you?"

"So, Nicky was in town today?" Oriole asked Summer.

"Yes," Summer said.

Sparrow looked at Oriole in surprise. "I told you," she said. "We took sandwiches and went to the beach, and Nicky went with us."

"Yes, I know, baby," Oriole said to Sparrow; and then definitely to Summer, she said, "Did you have a nice long rap?"

"Yeah. We had a nice long talk." She stared back, flat-eyed and unblinking, into Oriole's worried face. Oriole's eyes fell. "Where's your angelic friend today?" Summer asked. She'd meant to keep her voice neutral, but she knew she hadn't succeeded when Sparrow looked up quickly, her eyes anxious.

"Angelo went into Fort Bragg," Oriole said.

144

"Oh," Summer said. "Did any of the Fishers go with him? Just to be friendly, or anything. I guess they're all pretty good friends up there, spending so much time together and everything. I guess Angelo and the Fishers are pretty close friends by now?"

"I—I suppose so," Oriole said uneasily. "I don't know. I haven't talked to Galya very much lately. Like, everyone's so busy up there lately."

"You haven't talked to Galya?" Summer did an exaggeratedly amazed expression. "All that time at the Fishers', and you haven't talked to Galya?"

"Don't! Don't talk like that, Summer." Sparrow, who had been turning her worried face from one of them to the other as if she were watching a frighten-ening tennis match, suddenly ran to Summer and grabbed her arm. Looking up pleadingly, her artesian eyes already beginning to overflow, she begged, "Stop talking like that. Please."

Summer stopped. She hadn't meant to start an argument. In fact, what she'd intended to do was to be particularly friendly and chatty, to get Oriole off her guard. There was a lot of information she needed to get and that would require the best possible rapport between Oriole and herself; but somehow the sarcasm had just slipped out. For once she was glad for Spar-row's interruption. "Stop talking like what?" she said, smiling at Sparrow. "Nobody's arguing. Relax."

"Right on, baby." Oriole put down her sewing and jumped up. "War's over, so you can call off the protest march, little Peacenik." She rumpled Spar-row's head on her way to the kitchen. "Let's see what we can find for dinner. Okay?"

Summer cooled it after that; and all the time she was helping Oriole get dinner ready, warmed-up chicken stew and homemade bread, she made a special effort to be cheerful and friendly. At the table she even started a game that she and Oriole used to play with Sparrow, in which one person pretended to be a character from a fairy tale and the other two had to guess who they were. Sparrow was delighted, and Oriole threw herself into the game with all her usual enthusiasm for pretending—for pretending, not only that she was a fairy princess or a fire-breathing dragon, but also that everything was wonderful and beautiful when it was just the opposite. But the game served its purpose. Oriole forgot all about trying to find out if Nicky had ratted, and it wasn't until Sparrow had gone to bed that Summer started her own investigation.

Oriole had gone back to her sewing, and Summer was pretending to read a book as she figured out a plan of attack—an approach that might induce Oriole to reveal how much she knew about Angelo's relationship to the Fishers, as well as how she really felt about him. Summer had promised Nicky that she wouldn't tell Oriole about Angelo's threats and about Marina actually being a hostage. Nicky was sure that Oriole would tell Angelo—and then he would force her to go on talking until he knew exactly how she had found out. But Nicky might be wrong. Surely Oriole must be beginning to see Angelo for what he was, and a warning might be all it would take to get her to stay away from him. Planning her first careful question, Summer glanced up at Oriole, to find Oriole looking at her. As she opened her mouth to begin, Oriole said, "I suppose Nicky told you about the pot?"

It took a moment before Summer could manage to answer coolly. "No. Not really. That is, I already had it figured out."

Oriole nodded eagerly. "I was sure you had. I knew they were dumb, I mean, really out of it, to think my smart little Summer Baby wouldn't catch on." Her smile suddenly faded. "You won't say anything to anyone, will you. Like, it wouldn't be a good idea to let Angelo know that you're hip to what's happening up there."

Summer shrugged, hiding her sudden elation. Oriole had openly implied that Angelo was not only dangerous, but dumb. "Don't worry," she said, "I won't tell him anything. But will you?"

"No," Oriole said, quickly and firmly.

Summer couldn't help smiling. It was going well. "I've known about it for a long time," she said, "and I haven't told anyone. I just wish you weren't involved, though. What if there should be a raid, or something? Like that time in Round Valley when there was all that shooting and everything."

"Oh, baby." Oriole put down her sewing and stared at Summer. "You've been worrying again. You've always been such a worrier. There won't be any raid. Everyone knows about Galya's gardens and the greenhouses and everything. No one is going to get suspicious about Galya's famous berry farm."

"How come Galya let them do it?" Summer

147

asked. "She always said she'd never have anything to do with pot. How does she feel about it now?"

Oriole turned the yoke over to snip off a thread before she answered. "I'm not sure. At first, when she told me about it, she seemed to be all for it. You know. Excited about all the money and everything. But lately, I just don't know. She doesn't talk about it to me anymore. In fact, I haven't really rapped with Galya for a long time."

"But you're up there so much."

"I know. But I'm usually in the old cabin and Galya's busy in the house. But there've been times when—" Oriole's face, transparent as always, looked troubled. "I've asked her if she's down on me for some reason, and she says no, but—"

"Maybe she's down on Angelo," Summer said.

Oriole nodded thoughtfully. "Yes," she said. "I think she is. She hasn't said anything to me about it, but, you know, you can tell. Like, you know how friendly Galya always is to everyone, but she seems kind of uptight around Angelo. I guess it's to be expected. Probably Galya and Jerry are just tired of having so many extra people around all the time: Angelo and Bart and Jude. At first she was cooking for all of them, but lately the guys have been eating in the old cabin when I'm there to do the cooking. It's not easy for so many people to live more or less together for such a long time and not bum each other out. Even when you have an enlightened person like Esau there to keep everything mellow, like it was in the Tribe, it wasn't always easy. I remember once when this guy named Shadow, well actually his name was something like Arnold J. Something-or-other, but he called himself Shadow. Well, anyway, he got very uptight because . . ."

Oriole went on with the Angel Tribe story, babbling away as she had a thousand times before about the good old days when the flower children were in full bloom and everyone danced and sang and rapped about how love and mind-expansion and organic foods were going to change the face of the whole world. Summer tuned her out and considered what she had learned and what she ought to do next.

It seemed pretty obvious that Oriole didn't know the real situation between Angelo and the Fishers. If she had known, it all would have been right there in her face and voice. The question was, what would she do if she found out? Nicky, and probably the rest of the Fishers, thought it wouldn't be safe to tell her, because Angelo would get her to tell what she knew and who had told her. But maybe they were wrong. Maybe, if Oriole knew that the Creep was actually holding poor little Marina hostage, she'd come to her senses and stay away from him. Stay away from him and the Fishers and all the dangers that went with five big greenhouses full of pot. Suddenly, it seemed the only thing to do.

"Mother!"

Oriole's Angel Tribe anecdote stopped in mid-sentence. Her wide good-old-days-dreaming eyes narrowed with anxiety.

"Mother. Angelo is holding Marina hostage. Jerry and Galya didn't want to grow pot, not after they realized what they were getting into. And Angelo's making them go on with it. He says something's going to happen to Marina if the narcs find out about the crop."

Oriole looked stunned. She stared at Summer, blank-eyed, her pale freckles suddenly more noticeable against her white skin. "That's crazy," she said, "I don't believe it." She shook her head slowly, and then covered her face with her hands. Summer sat stiffly, wanting to comfort her one moment, and the next to yell at her and ask her how she could have been such a fool. It was several minutes before Oriole lifted her head. "I asked Galya," she said, "about Marina. She told me she had to stay in the house because of the pollens. She told me it was the doctor's orders."

Summer waited. She didn't have to say anymore. Oriole was saying it herself. "One of them's always in the house. Angelo usually stays in the old cabin, but if the other two are both out, he goes to the house." There was another long pause, and she said, "He takes his gun. He takes his gun when he goes to the big cabin." She sighed so deeply it was almost a moan, and then lapsed into silence. Summer went on waiting—waiting for Oriole to realize what she had done and to decide what she would do now that she knew the truth. They were both still sitting silently a moment later when feet pounded on the steps, the door banged open, and Angelo came into the trailer.

He stood in the doorway grinning, his eyes quick and busy. Oriole, still sitting with her forgotten sewing in her lap, stared up at him, her face expressionless. "You ready?" he said. "Come on. I got to get

150

back. I've been gone all day. I got some nice big T-bones. You wouldn't want me to have to cook them myself, would you."

When Oriole started to get to her feet, Summer grabbed her arm. "She can't go," she said. "She can't go tonight."

"Well, well. Would you listen to this. Look who's got her voice back. And look who's telling her own mother what she can't do."

"She can't go tonight because of Sparrow," Summer said. "She's sick."

The quick eyes flicked to Summer and back to Oriole. "Sure." His face was cold. "Sure she is. And her gabby big sister's just the one to play nursemaid 'til her mommy gets home. You can do that, can't you? I'll bet you could do it better than your poor little skinny mom, if you tried real hard."

He grinned then, the grin that was even more threatening that his scowl. "Matter of fact, I wouldn't be surprised if there was a lot of things you could do better than your old lady. Like cooking steaks, for instance. How'd you like to come up and cook my steaks tonight so your poor old lady can stay home with her sick kid. How about that? Might be a real nice change for everybody." He looked at Oriole and his voice had an edge like a razor blade as he said, "Matter of fact, the way things have been going lately, I've been thinking about making a change or two."

"Let's go," Oriole said. "I'm ready." She unwrapped Summer's fingers from around her arm. She wouldn't look at Summer as she got her sweater and went out the door. But Angelo looked back at her—running his eyes slowly down over her body and then back up again. Then he grinned again and stomped out, leaving the door open. The night breeze blew into the room and flickered the flame in the propane lamp, but it was a long time before it blew away the scent of stale aftershave lotion.

12

Oriole refuses to talk to me about it. Ever since the night I told her about Marina's being a hostage and she went off with the Creep anyway, she just won't answer me when I try to talk about it. I tried again tonight. I begged her to at least stop going up to the Fishers', because of what might happen if there should be a raid. The Creep could still come here to see her. I said that even though my job at the Pardells' is ending, I'd take Sparrow and go to town everyday so they could have the trailer to themselves, if she just wouldn't go up there anymore. But she wouldn't answer. She just stared at me with a miserable expression on her face, as if she was about to start crying, and said she wouldn't talk about it.

I don't think it's an act. A lot of the time she looks even more miserable when she doesn't know I'm watching. Miserable and *frightened. I really think that ever since she found out what's going on between Angelo and the Fishers, she's been scared to death, but for some reason she won't do anything about it. There are things we could do, like going away, for instance. I've tried to tell her that we could pack up and go to some other town, but she just says we can't because we don't have any money. I told her about my bank account. She wouldn't believe me until I got my bankbook and showed her how much I have. Then she said that it wasn't enough because if we moved it would take so long to get back on AFDC and food stamps. But I don't think money's the real problem. I think the real problem is that down deep she doesn't want to go. Oh she's scared, all right. But, in a way, that's one reason she won't go. There's a part of Oriole that wants to be scared—scared and helpless and in danger. I don't know why. I don't see why anyone in their right mind would want to feel that way, but this isn't the first time it's happened. It's not the first time that Oriole has gotten involved with somebody who turned out to be dangerous in one way or another. The Creep is the worst maybe, but not the first.*

The other problem is that she's been smoking a lot of pot again. She says she hasn't, but I can always tell because her eyes get red and her voice gets slow and slurry.

*She always smokes her brains out whenever
things get really bad. At least she does if she
can get it, and she sure hasn't had any trouble getting it lately.*

"Hey, look at this one. Look at this one, Summer.
Isn't this a good father?" Sparrow plunked a *Ladies
Home Journal* down on the table right on top of the
letter Summer was writing. "Just look, he's got all his
feet and everything, and he's just the right size."
Sparrow was cutting paper dolls out of old magazines and apparently having a lot of trouble finding
enough pictures of complete figures. Particularly
men, it seemed. Or else she was just providing some
spare fathers for her paper doll families. Which
wouldn't be surprising, when you came to think about
it. In Sparrow's experience, a rapid turnover in fathers was par for the course.

"Very nice," Summer said. The father in question
was very tan and handsome and part of an ad for
suntan lotion. "Not especially fatherly, but nice.
You'll have to draw some clothes on him, won't you?"

"Or they can live at the beach," Sparrow said.
"I'll just play like they live at the beach, and he won't
need to have clothes on." Picking up her *Ladies
Home Journal* she went back to where she'd been
sitting in the middle of the floor, surrounded by a
huge stack of old magazines that she'd bummed off of
Nan Oliver. And Summer went back to her letter.

*I guess the Olivers will be leaving soon.
They finally sold the ranch, and tomorrow
Nan is going back east with Richard to help*

155

decide which place they're going to buy. Then she'll come back here just long enough to finish selling the horses and a lot of other stuff and do the packing. I'll be working there every day for a while, helping pack and clean, but then that job will be over, too. I still haven't told Nan that I'm not going with them. Actually though, I've never told her I was, either. I just said I was still thinking about it, and she took it for granted that that meant yes. I'll have to tell her soon, but I keep putting it off because I want to go on working as long as possible, and I have a feeling she's going to get really angry when she finds out I'm turning down her magnificent offer. Last Saturday she asked me again if Oriole would let me go, and I said she would. She would, too, if I asked her. That is, she might object at first, but I could talk her into it, if I wanted to.

Last weekend Sparrow stayed overnight at the Olivers. They were having important guests for dinner who were bringing a kid about Sparrow's age, and Nan thought it would be nice if the kid had someone to play with. Or maybe it was Richard who thought so, because he seemed to be all for the idea. Sparrow had a great time. Nan bought her an old fashioned ruffles-and-lace type dress for the occasion, and she and the other kid ate with the grown-ups and Elmira waited on the table. They had some kind of fancy

156

flaming dessert served on a big silver platter.
Sparrow came home acting like Cinderella
returning from the prince's ball and asking
stupid questions like how come we didn't
ever set things on fire before we ate them. It
took her two days to get down to earth again
and stop strutting around like a peacock. It
probably would have taken her longer, ex-
cept I told her that the Olivers were going
away. I was pretty tired of the royal high-
ness bit. But after I told her, she cried for
two hours and I wished I hadn't. But so
what, she would have had to find out sooner
or later, and it might as well be sooner. Now
it's over with.

That was one good thing about Sparrow—she
always got over things quickly. Just the day before
she'd been acting as if she were about to die of grief,
wailing about how she loved the ranch and the horses
and the peacocks and Nan and Richard more than
anything in the world and if they went away she was
going to die. Now here she was, perfectly happy,
arranging a ridiculous assortment of makeshift paper
dolls along the edge of the lounge. Chewing on the
end of her pen, Summer studied Sparrow critically.
She'd put on her nightgown right after dinner and
announced dramatically that she was going to go to
bed and cry herself to sleep. That had been before
she'd remembered her plan to look through the magazines for paper dolls. So here she was, two hours
later, sitting on the floor in her favorite nightgown,

breathing. Summer slipped from the bed, and moving quietly to the door, she slid the thin wood panel an inch to the right. Putting her eye to the crack she peered through into a blinding beam of light. The door moved again, in a sharp jerk, and a rough hand grabbed her shoulder and pulled her forward into the living room.

There were two of them. Two men carrying flashlights and pistols. The one who was holding her shone the flashlight into her face, and as she jumped back, blinded and terrified, his grip tightened. "Hey. Hey," he said. "Calm down. Nobody's going to hurt you. Who else is here, in the trailer?"

She struggled again, but the man's grip on her forearm was firm and strong. "Cool it, kid," he said. "Just answer my question. Are you alone?"

"Yes," she gasped. "Alone. I'm alone."

He went on holding her while the other man crossed into the hallway that led to the bathroom and Oriole's bedroom. In a moment he was back. "No one there," he said and headed toward Summer's room.

"Don't," she said. "Don't go in there." He paused for a second and then he raised his gun and disappeared into the bedroom. Summer was still struggling, trying to follow him, when he reappeared, grinning. "Just a sleeping kid," he said. "Thought you said you were alone, little lady."

"I am. Except for my little sister. We're here alone."

"They must be up the hill, with the others," the man who was holding Summer said. "Looks like we're on a wild goose chase."

160

It wasn't until then that she noticed what she must have seen before and was too much in shock to understand. The two men were wearing uniforms. For a brief moment the terror subsided, but an instant later it returned, in a smothering surge of fear. It was a raid. The men were narcs, and they were looking for Angelo. They would go on up the hill and find him, and there would be the narcs with their guns and Angelo with his. And Oriole. She clawed at the fingers holding her arm, trying to break away to run out the door and up the road, to run and run until she found Oriole.

"Hey, cut that out,' the narc said, but she went on struggling until Sparrow appeared in the doorway, Oriole's black nightgown sliding off one shoulder, her eyes wide with fright.

"Summer," Sparrow's wail was a counter-force, stemming the dark tide.

"It's all right," Summer told her. "They won't hurt us. They're looking for someone else." She held out her arms, and Sparrow threw herself into them sobbing.

Comforting Sparrow, trying to tell her everything would be all right, Summer was only vaguely aware of the rumbling voices of the intruders until one of them, a big, heavy man with a saggy face, came out of the bedroom with Sparrow's shoes. "Hurry up, ladies," he said. "Get some clothes on. We're taking you with us."

On the path one of the men walked ahead and one behind, the heavy tread of their booted feet loud in the midnight stillness. Between them Sparrow

161

trudged obediently, clinging to Summer's hand and occasionally shuddering with stifled sobs. It was Sparrow's hand, small and cold and shaking, that held back the dark wave and kept the tightness in Summer's stomach from turning into sharp, burning pain. Holding on tightly, Summer kept whispering, "It's all right. Everything's going to be all right," a desperate invocation against fear, her own as well as Sparrow's.

A patrol car was parked on the Fishers' road, near the beginning of the path—white and black, lights flashing from the roof, an iron grill between the front and back seats. One of the men got into the driver's seat while the other opened the back door and boosted Sparrow in. It was then, in the moment that his back was turned, that her fear surged up—and she ran.

Barely aware of the shouts and the thudding feet behind her, she sped up the road to the first break in the heavy underbrush. A few feet into the clustering bushes and saplings she threw herself to the ground, crawling under the sprawling branches of a huge rhododendron. When the sound of pursuit had retreated, she ran again.

She was scrambling up a footpath between switchbacks when the noise of a motor warned her, and flattening herself between boulders on the steep slope, she watched as the patrol car went by below her, rounded the sharp turn and passed by again above her head. Back on the roadway, she went on running.

It was not long afterwards that she heard the shots —a single sharp report and then three or four more in rapid succession. For a moment her stride broke

162

and she stumbled and fell. She struggled to a sitting position, and vaguely aware of the pain in her hands and knees, she strained to hear over the noisy rasp of her breath. Silence. Back on her feet, she ran again, slower now as she fought the painful exhaustion in her lungs and legs.

Not far beyond the switchbacks, the sound of another approaching car drove her off the road again, quickly this time as the noise swelled rapidly to a threatening roar. Someone was driving fast, ignoring the danger of sharp turns on slippery gravel. With barely time to find cover, Summer darted behind a spindly sapiling, hoping desperately that its thin branches would block the probing headlights. Rounding the last turn the vehicle accelerated quickly and sped past, a large white van with flashing lights, and large blue letters across its doors. An ambulance.

"Oriole." The name was a pain that throbbed through her head as she began to run again. "Oriole. Oriole."

The gate was wide open. The yard in front of the house was full of cars and people. Patrol cars were everywhere. Near the veranda steps the ambulance was parked, its rear doors open. Lights were blazing —glaring, blinding light—spilling from the windows and from the headlights of all of the cars. A group of people were clustered near a van, and the air was full of the sound of voices, talking and shouting. Inside the ambulance a white-coated figure was bending over a blanket-draped figure on one of the litters. Summer had started forward when two men came out of the house and down the stairs carrying a

163

stretcher. "Oriole. Oriole." Her lips shaped the words, but her throat refused to respond as she lurched into a staggering run. But the person who lay on the stretcher, his face contorted with pain, was Adam Fisher.

"Watch it," someone said as Summer's knees weakened suddenly and she clutched at the edge of the stretcher. And then, "Hey. Where'd you come from? Christ! Looks like we got another wounded. Joe! Joe! Can you take care of this one."

"It's all right," Summer said. "I just fell down." The blood on her arms and legs seemed unreal, faint and far away. The white coated man was receding, too, even as he walked toward her, his voice growing soft and distant. As the world reeled past, blurred and fluid, only one small segment of the fading scene came through sharp and clear—the sight of Oriole coming down the veranda steps. Oriole, upright and unbloodied, smiling up at the big policeman who was leading her down the stairs. Then the darkness closed down.

13

"Well, so much for Charlie Brown." Fritzie, a twelve-year-old child-abuse case from Willits, threw her comic book across the room and sat up. "They never get anything worth reading in this dump, like *Zaps* or *Slow Death*." Getting off her bunk she came over to peer down at the beat up copy of *The Diary of Anne Frank* that Summer was reading. "You like that?"

"It's okay," Summer said. "I read it before, a long time ago. But I couldn't find anything else that looked good, so I thought I'd read it again."

"It's sad, isn't it? I was supposed to read it last year in school, but I didn't because I don't like to read sad stuff."

Fritzie, who was in a children's shelter home for the third time because her father had beaten her up, had pale, empty eyes and a big bruise on her left cheek. Last night, after Sparrow and Marina were sound asleep, she sat on the side of Summer's bunk for a long time, comparing the various children's shelter homes and the beatings that had caused her to be in them. She went into a great deal of detail about both, her pale eyes inward and unfocused. Summer felt she could get up and walk away, or even turn into some kind of grotesque monster, and Fritzie would go right on talking without noticing. It seemed that the beatings, as well as the foster homes, were gradually getting worse. The food was a lot better where she'd been last time, she said, than here at the Jensens', and the Jensens were real uptight about TV watching—no sex or violence. Fritzie liked violence on TV.

"They're going! Jerry and Galya came and they're going to take Marina and Nicky away." Sparrow burst into the room, slammed the door behind her and stood leaning against it, staring at Summer accusingly—as if it were somehow her fault. Fritzie went back and flopped on her bunk. Leaning on one elbow she listened openly, but with limited interest, as if she were watching a dull soap opera.

Summer shrugged. "Nicky told you," she said. "He said their lawyer had arranged for bail and they would all be going home today."

"What's bail?" Sparrow asked.

"It's money somebody pays; they don't get it back if the person who got arrested doesn't show up in court when they're supposed to. So then the person who got arrested gets to go home until time for their trial."

"Will somebody pay bail for us so we can go home?"

"Not for us, silly. We didn't get arrested."

166

"Yes, we did. When those two policemen came. Wasn't that arrested?"

"No! They just took us into protective custody. Nicky and Marina, too. Only now Jerry and Galya are out on bail, so Nicky and Marina get to go home."

"Oh. I get it." Sparrow drifted across the room, obviously deep in thought, and collapsed on the bed next to where Summer was sitting. She was on the track, now, and Summer could guess what would be coming next. The question came—right on schedule. "When is Oriole going to be bailed?"

Across the room Fritzie was still listening. "I don't know for sure," Summer told Sparrow. "But it'll probably be pretty soon."

"Today?"

"Well, maybe not today. But it might be tomorrow. I kind of have a feeling it might be tomorrow."

"Really?" Sparrow looked delighted. Jumping to her feet, she ran for the door. "I want to tell Marina. Maybe they haven't gone yet. I'm going to go see if they've gone."

When Sparrow had gone, Fritzie sat up. "Hey kid," she said, "what's your old lady in for anyway?"

"I don't want to talk about it. Okay?" Summer turned her back and picked up her book. But Fritzie wasn't easily squelched.

"It must have been a real big one if they won't let her out on bail. When my dad put my mom and me both in the hospital, they let him out on bail."

"I thought you didn't have any mother." Summer said.

"Well, I did then. A stepmother anyway. But she split, too, after that. But what about your mom? Was it murder? Did your old lady kill somebody?"

This time Summer didn't say anything. Holding her book in front of her face, she tuned Frizie out and thought about the reasons the Fishers had been released on bail, and the possibility that Oriole might not.

Oriole's situation wasn't at all the same as the Fishers'. For one thing they were landowners and that made a big difference. And then there was the fact that the Fishers had tried to get out of the pot deal and had been forced to continue because Marina was being held as a hostage. At first Summer had wondered if the police would believe the Fishers' story about the hostage thing; but yesterday when Nicky had talked to the lawyer, he'd heard some good news. First, there had been a test that proved that the bullet in Adam's shoulder had come from Angelo's gun, and then Jude had broken down and told the truth about Angelo's threats.

So the bail had been reduced, and the Fishers had been allowed to go home, which meant that Nicky and Marina could leave the children's shelter. But Oriole's bail had not been reduced, and in spite of what she'd told Sparrow, Summer wasn't at all sure when the McIntyres would be going home. As far as the police were concerned, Oriole was Angelo's girl friend and, as such, one of the criminals who was being charged not only with growing pot, but also of hostage-taking, resisting arrest and because of Adam and a wounded policeman, attempted manslaughter.

The Fishers might be able to help by testifying that Oriole wasn't really involved, but according to Nicky, Jerry and Galya felt that Oriole had betrayed their friendship by taking up with Angelo. So the chances that Oriole would be released soon didn't look at all good.

There was a knock on the door, and Mrs. Jensen came into the room carrying a big cardboard box. She put the box down on the foot of Summer's bed. "Mrs. Fisher," she said, answering Summer's unspoken question. "She said to tell you she went by your house and picked up some clothing for you and Sparrow. And they'd like to see you before they go."

Summer got to her feet slowly. Under the heavy bandages, her knees were still stiff and painful, but there was more than physical discomfort behind her lack of haste. She felt very strange about seeing Galya and Jerry again. Although there were a lot of questions she desperately wanted to ask them, she knew she wouldn't have the nerve. How do you ask someone about a close friend who turned out to be a traitor, particularly if the traitor happened to be your mother?

In the Jensens' large, comfortably shabby living room, the Fishers were waiting. Galya and Jerry were standing near the door. Nicky was sprawled on one of the couches, and in the corner, Marina and Sparrow were clutching each others' hands and looking tragic.

"Summer, honey." Galya's jangling bracelets and smothering hugs were the same as always, and even Jerry's normal scowl seemed a little more benevolent

169

than usual. "Now don't you worry," Galya was saying. "We're going to do everything we can to see that you and Sparrow get home real soon. We're working on it, aren't we, Jerry?"

It seemed that whether or not the Fishers had forgiven Oriole for taking up with Angelo, they weren't holding it against Summer and Sparrow. But nothing was said about Oriole, and there was no opportunity to ask questions. Releasing Summer from her hug, Galya swooped down on Sparrow; Sparrow and Marina began to cry in unison, and Jerry disappeared out the door. In the total confusion that followed, Nicky was suddenly standing beside Summer.

"Hang in there,' he said. "Everything's going to be all right." He kissed her so quickly she didn't even have time to decide whether or not to kiss back. He went out the door, and a moment later the Fishers were gone, Sparrow was sobbing in the corner, and Mrs. Jensen was bustling through the room with a dustmop.

Back in their room, Summer comforted Sparrow and got her started playing with some plastic horses before she went out into the back yard. The Jensens, whose own kids were now grown up, had a kid oriented yard—large and dusty and full of beat-up play equipment. Pulling a lounge chair into the shade of the high wall, Summer stretched out on her stomach, her book propped in front of her. She read page fifteen over three times before she gave up.

She'd been trying not to think. It had been easy at first. When they'd first arrived at the Jensens' custodial home, early yesterday morning, she'd been groggy from being up almost all night and from the pain pills the ambulance attendant had insisted she take before he cleaned and bandaged her knees and elbows. She'd fallen asleep immediately and awakened hours later, feeling woozy and unreal. The rest of that first day had slipped by like a half-remembered dream—meals in the big family room, being chatted at by the grandmotherly Mrs. Jensen and the constant confusion of the Jensens' girls' room, where Sparrow and Marina were staging a dramatic day-long celebration of their reunion and Fritzie was always on the lookout for a sounding board for her personal horror stories. When the day was finally over, darkness had brought quick and long-lasting oblivion.

This morning, right after breakfast, there'd been the talk with Nicky. When she'd started to leave the family room with Sparrow, he'd asked her to stay; and when they were alone, he'd moved to the chair next to hers. He wanted to talk about Adam.

It wasn't surprising that Adam and Nicky had disagreed about what to do about Angelo, since they had always disagreed about everything; but this time it had almost cost Adam his life. Nicky had wanted to go to the police, but Adam had said it would be too dangerous because it would be impossible to know where everyone would be and what they would be doing when the raid started. His plan was for the Fishers to take care of Angelo themselves. They would steal a gun—Bart was often careless with his—and get the drop on Angelo.

"It was crazy," Nicky said. *"Shoot Out at the OK*

Corral, with Adam and me being the guys in the white hats. Just like we used to play when we were kids, only this time with real guns and bullets. But Adam—God, Summer—he didn't seem to be afraid at all. He kept insisting we could do it, if I'd help him."

But Nicky wouldn't agree. And neither of them could talk to Jerry about it because he was too frightened about what might happen to Marina. So then Nicky had decided to take matters into his own hands. Last week when it had again been his turn to go into town and do his "everything's normal at the Fishers' act," he'd called the sheriff's office.

"Why didn't you tell me?" Summer had asked. "You promised."

"I promised I'd try to," Nicky said. "I went to Pardells' looking for you, but you weren't there. And then Angelo took me home. There was no way I could get to the trailer; and besides, what good would it have done if I'd told you. I couldn't tell you when the raid would be, because I didn't know."

It was the truth, or at least a part of it. But of course the other part was that Nicky had been afraid of what would have happened if she'd told Oriole. Afraid that Oriole would have betrayed her oldest and best friends to her latest lover.

After that, for a little while, Summer found it hard to listen; but as Nicky went on, his face tense with horror, she found herself living the raid as he had lived it. Just as he had feared, both Angelo and Bart had been in the house when it began. There was the screeching of an alarm and a sudden roaring bark

172

from the doberman, followed almost immediately by
Jude pounding up the steps and into the house. And
then Adam had grabbed Jude's gun, and Jude had his
hands up and was begging Adam not to shoot him
and saying how he hadn't wanted to do anything to
hurt the Fishers, but Angelo had made him do it.
Then Angelo came in the door, and when Adam
turned toward him—Angelo had fired. Nicky had
seen Adam fall, and it wasn't until much later when
it was all over, with Angelo wounded by police gun-
fire and in custody along with Bart and Jude, that he
learned that Adam would not die.

"How long was that?" she asked. "Until it was all
over?"

"I don't know for sure. Maybe only a half hour."
Nicky's eyes looked blind—as if they were still seeing
nothing except that long thirty minutes. His voice
caught as he said, "It seemed like—forever."

It was obvious that Nicky blamed himself for
what happened to Adam. His familiar face, deep-
eyed and lean like Jerry's, but with Galya's wide, full-
lipped mouth, looked suddenly much older. Older
and full of pain. Of course Summer told him that he
shouldn't blame himself, that if he'd agreed to try
Adam's plan, things might have turned out much
worse. He wasn't ready to listen yet, but she told him
anyhow. And then, without knowing she was going
to, she kissed him. It was a very short kiss because the
Jensens' family room was about as private as Grand
Central Station, but it seemed to do more good than
anything she'd been able to say.

But now the Fishers were back home and only

Summer and Sparrow were still at the Jensens', along with Bobby, whose mother had abandoned him, and Fritzie, whose father beat her with a broom handle. It was anybody's guess how long they would have to stay. There could be days and days in the Jensens' Naugahyde family room eating Wonder Bread and fried potatoes and watching *Lawrence Welk* and *Walt Disney Presents* on the TV, and endless nights in the "girls' room" with its linoleum floor that smelled of disinfectant and three sets of metal bunk beds, while other kids whose parents were in jail or who beat them, came and went and—like Fritzie— came again.

Whose parents were in jail . . . Summer rolled over on her back and put her arm across her eyes, trying to shut out a picture of Oriole. A picture of Oriole alone in a dark cell—a cell from an illustration in a book she'd once read—perhaps, *Les Miserables* or *The Count of Monte Cristo*. Stone walls, a narrow bunk and a tiny barred window, with the ragged, bearded figure of the illustration replaced by another thin, pale prisoner, her face furrowed with deep wrinkles and her bright hair turned thin and gray. Other pictures came then—Oriole playing games with Sparrow on the trailer floor—singing "Gentle on My Mind" as she kneaded bread at the kitchen table—on a picnic with flowers in her hair.

She sat up suddenly, her fists clenched. The summoned anger flamed like an opened furnace, burning away the tears that had started to flood her eyes. "Damn her," she whispered. "God damn her."

It wasn't until then that she suddenly thought of

174

the Olivers. In all the time, almost thirty-six hours since the raid had started, the Olivers had not entered her mind. Away in Connecticut buying their new home, they had disappeared from her thoughts as well. But now suddenly they returned, just as they would return before long to gather up all their many belongings and leave Alvarro Bay forever. And just as suddenly Summer knew what she was going to do.

It was no more than fifteen minutes later, and she was still sitting on the edge of the lounge chair, thinking and planning, when Mrs. Jensen appeared at the back door.

"Summer," she called. "Come here. You have visitors."

She couldn't think who it might be, and under the circumstances she certainly couldn't think whom she would want it to be. She supposed most of Alvarro Bay knew by now about what had happened, so it might be almost anyone. She hoped it wouldn't be someone like Haley and her mother, full of condolences and curiosity.

For some reason she never thought of the Pardells until she walked into the living room, although as soon as she heard what they were there for, she wasn't at all surprised. It was just like Meg and Pardell to take on two more stray cats and then pretend to blame each other for it.

14

The scene at the Food Mart was just about what she'd expected. It was the first time she'd been downtown since she and Sparrow had moved in with the Pardells, and left to her own devices, she'd have put it off even longer. In another week or two, some other local scandal might have occurred to take people's minds off the big pot bust at the Fishers'. So when Meg said she needed help with the shopping because of the crutches, Summer was anything but enthusiastic. She'd even thought of offering Sparrow's services, but Marina had just arrived for a visit so that was out. She'd agreed to go very reluctantly.

"I really appreciate this, Summer," Meg said as they were pulling up in front of the Mart. "And I'm sure Arnie will, too. After last week, I've been afraid he was about to revoke my license to operate a grocery cart in his store."

"Why? What happened last week?"

"I had one of those wobbly wheeled carts, and when I tried to turn the corner with one hand, it went out of control and sideswiped a display of strawberry jam. Then, while I was grabbing at falling jam jars, I dropped my crutch and clobbered a small fortune's worth of instant coffee."

So, of course, Summer said she was glad to help, and while Meg concentrated on her shopping, Summer pushed the grocery cart and tried to ignore the stares. Since it was midweek, most of the shoppers were local people, and it was immediately apparent that everyone in Alvarro Bay knew all about the raid and everybody involved. The stares varied from curious to hostile to sympathetic. As usual, it was the sympathetic that she hated most. If Arnie had only known ahead of time, he could have advertised. "All you locals who've enjoyed feeling sorry for the poor McIntyre kids all these years, drop in tomorrow for a real bargain basement special."

She hadn't thought Meg had noticed, but when they were on the way home, she suddenly said, "It takes a thick hide, doesn't it? That's the way with life in a small town. There's no comfortable shell of anonymity, so we all have to grow our own." She leaned over then and patted Summer's arm. "But don't let it get too thick, honey. There'll be times and places when it won't be necessary any longer."

Summer nodded, smiling stiffly. "I know," she said. And to herself she added that her own time for small towns, and the thick hides they made necessary, would be over very soon, if everything worked out according to her plans.

As they pulled into the yard, Pardell was playing football on the front lawn with Sparrow and Marina and Patrick, the eight-year-old kid from next door. Pardell was flat on his face under a stack of squirming kids, but when he saw the car he got up and walked over to the driveway, with Sparrow and Marina still clinging to him like a couple of leeches.

"Alan," Meg said. "I thought you were going to get some work done this afternoon while the girls were out of the study."

Pardell grinned. "That was the plan, wasn't it. But first things first. My duty as an educator called, and I answered."

"An educator?"

"Absolutely. Sparrow and Marina came in for a little chat, and I discovered that their education has been sadly neglected. Here they are pushing eight years old and completely ignorant of the basic principles of the great sport of football."

"But they're little girls," Meg said.

Pardell looked down at the kids and raised his shaggy eyebrows in a surprised expression—as if he'd just noticed. "Well, so they are," he said. "But a pair of promising first string tackles, nevertheless." He shook his leg gently, detaching Marina who was still clutching his ankle. "Okay, team. On your feet. The play's over." He tossed the football to Patrick. "Call the next play, quarterback, while I take in the groceries."

It wasn't until he came into the kitchen with the last two bags that he suddenly thumped his forehead and said. "I nearly forgot. You got some mail, Summer. A letter and a poscard. On the dining room table."

178

The letter was postmarked Ukiah and was addressed to Summer in Oriole's disjointed, childish handwriting. Summer took it into her room, or rather into Pardell's study, before she opened it.

My Beautiful Babies,

I've just heard the news. I've always thought that Meg and Alan Pardell were just about the most beautiful people in Alvarro Bay, and now I know it. I'm so happy and relieved. I was really freaking out, sitting here all day thinking about my Beautiful Babies shut up in some kind of Kiddie Jail just because their dumb mother doesn't know how to pick her friends.

Don't worry about me. This place isn't exactly the Taj Mahal, but it's not as bad as it could be. The food's pretty plastic but there's plenty of it, and there are books to read and once in a while even TV. I've been talking to Greg Allbright, he's the Fishers' lawyer and he's going to represent me, too. Isn't that great! He's a great lawyer and a really beautiful human being, and Galya is going to take care of his fee for the time being and I'll pay her back later. Greg thinks that I'll be a good witness and that the jury will see that I wasn't really involved in what was going on at the Fishers', and find me not guilty.

I miss you both like crazy, and I'm really counting the days until we're all back again in our trailer in the free, clean forest air.

 Summer, why don't you get a dozen real nice roses and give them to Meg Pardell from me and tell her how much I appreciate what she's doing. And maybe you could ask her if she's coming to Ukiah to bring you kids along so we could have a visit. It may be a few weeks yet before the trial comes up, and I'm really going to be climbing the walls if I don't get to see my babies before then.

 Hoping to see you real soon,
     Your loving Oriole

Summer put the letter down quickly to keep from wadding it into a ball and throwing it across the room. She wanted to scream. She wanted to scream things about free air, and lawyers and roses that weren't free. And babies that weren't either. That shouldn't be, at least, because after a while they stopped being babies and definitely stopped being free. But she didn't scream because she couldn't without scaring a lot of people to death. In a house as small as the Pardells', you couldn't scream, and you couldn't stay for very long either. Not when you had to sleep on a hide-a-bed in somebody's study so that most of the time he couldn't even get to his desk.

It was several minutes before she trusted herself to put the letter back in the envelope. She'd forgotten all about the postcard, but when she picked up the envelope there it was. It was from Nan Oliver and it said that she and Richard would be back in Alvarro Bay at the end of the week.

That was on Wednesday, and on Thursday Summer went with Sparrow to the Fishers'. Galya had been driving in to town every morning to leave Marina at the Pardells' or to pick up Sparrow. But when she arrived on Thursday, Nicky was with her. Summer was weeding the flower garden, and while Galya was in the house collecting Sparrow, he strolled over and stood around watching. After they'd both said "hi," Summer went on weeding while she waited to see what was coming next. She was beginning to think nothing was, when Nicky said, "You want to play *Star Wars?* You can be Darth Vader."

In the old days who got to be Darth Vader was one of the things they always fought over. She sat back on her heels and looked at him. "You mean I don't have to wrestle you for it?" she asked.

"Not unless you want to," he said, and then he grinned and raised his right hand and said it again. "Not unless you want to."

It seemed very strange to be at the Fishers' again. It was the first time in more than six months, except for the night of the raid and the other night visit when she'd come looking for Sparrow. Adam was home from the hospital with his arm in a sling, looking palely heroic and taking himself even more seriously than ever. Jerry and Galya and Nicky were busy preparing the huge greenhouses, five of them now, for some new varieties of berries; and Sparrow and Marina were in a seventh heaven of imaginary adventures and giggly secrets.

181

Most of the day Summer helped out in the greenhouses, but in the afternoon she accepted Nicky's invitation to go for a hike in the woods. It was a cool day, with a high, thin overcast filtering the sunlight and a slight tang of surf and spray in the breeze. They followed a deer trail to the top of the ridge to where they could see clear down to the town and beyond it to the dim line where the sea met the sky. Near the highest point of the trail, they found a fallen log and sat down to rest.

When Nicky put his arm around her shoulders, Summer didn't resist; but when she took his other hand and held it, it was partly to keep it under control. She remembered his hands as almost as small as hers, with close-bitten grubby nails and scraped and scabby knuckles. But the hand she was holding was large and lean and masculine, with long sensitive-looking fingers. She thought of saying something about the change; but when she looked up at him, he started to kiss her. She pulled away instinctively, but he stopped and said, "Okay, Darth. You got it." So after a few minutes she looked up at him again.

They'd tried several kinds of kisses, and Summer had found that she liked most of them when Nicky started talking about next year at school and what the reaction was going to be to a Fisher-McIntyre item, and how she felt about going, not steady, which was pretty passé, but at least fairly steadily. As she listened, Summer went stiff and silent, and when he finally noticed and asked her what was the matter, she had to tell him.

He didn't believe her at first, and then he said he didn't understand it, and then he got angry and said, and what was he supposed to do, and what in the hell did she think Oriole was going to do when she got out of jail.

And then suddenly she was very angry, and she told him that Oriole would go right on doing what she'd always done and anyway it wasn't any of his business. Then she got up and ran down the path. He caught up with her after a while, but she refused to talk to him. They went all the rest of the way down the hill in silence.

When they got back to the Fishers', Galya was getting ready to leave for Alvarro Bay. Before they left, Summer reminded Nicky that she'd told him about her plan in strictest confidence and asked him not to mention it to anyone. "Okay," he said. "But I don't see why it matters. They'll all know soon enough, anyway."

"Maybe not. It may not happen."

"Oh yeah? Well, wouldn't that be too bad. That would be a real disappointment, wouldn't it?"

Nicky's sarcasm usually drove her up the wall, but for some reason she didn't flare up this time. There was something in his face that revealed the pain that lay beneath his anger, and anger that hurt was something Summer knew a lot about.

"I don't want to go," she told him, and it was at least partly true.

"Then why are you? Why can't you just stay at the Pardells'?"

"They really haven't room for us. And besides, they're planning to take a year off and live in Europe soon."

Galya came out of the house then with Sparrow, and there wasn't time to say anymore. As they drove away, Nicky was still standing on the front veranda, but when Summer waved, he didn't wave back.

On the way home they stopped to let Summer and Sparrow get some things they needed from the trailer. While Galya waited in the car, they ran down the familiar path for the first time since the raid. Although it had only been about a week, there was a deserted look to the clearing, and inside the trailer the air smelled dusty and dead. Summer couldn't wait to get out. She threw some things into shopping bags, clothing and shoes and a few of Sparrow's favorite toys. In the bottom of the biggest bag she put Grant's hairbrush and the letter box.

On Saturday Nan Oliver called. They'd gotten home that morning, and as soon as they found Summer's note, they'd called the Pardells'. Nan sounded shocked and horrified.

"How perfectly awful for poor little Sparrow," she said. "For you both—but Sparrow's at such an impressionable age." Sparrow was impressionable all right; but although Summer didn't say so, she felt certain that having an only parent put in jail just might make as much of a dent in a sixteen-year-old. In her experience seven-year-olds bounced back. Like Silly Putty they could be all out of shape one minute and back to normal the next. But she didn't argue.

"We'd like to see you," she said, and less than an

hour later the dark blue Cadillac pulled up in front of the Pardells'.

She almost didn't do it. It was something about the precise orderliness of the long, low ranch house, even now in the midst of packing. Along the walls identical boxes of carefully wrapped treasures were perfectly aligned, and there wasn't a scrap of paper or trace of dust anywhere. Things weren't where they used to be. The carefully designed patterns had changed. But there were still patterns, and for some reason, they were more noticeable than ever. She'd not minded it before. In fact the predictability and stability of everything at Crown Ridge had seemed pleasant and comfortable. But now, suddenly, she found herself wondering what the Olivers' patterns would create from the seven-year-old Silly Putty that was Sparrow.

But of course Nan and Richard had wanted to hear all about the raid and Oriole's involvement; and explaining it—even explaining it in words that told as little as possible—reminded Summer of her plan. So while they were having tea and pastries on the patio, and Sparrow had temporarily disappeared across the lawn after the peacocks, she made her proposal.

She did it straight out front this time, without any pretense or subterfuge. She simply asked them if they'd like to have Sparrow, and when they said they would, she told them how to go about it.

15

She couldn't sleep. And when she finally did, she kept dreaming things that woke her up with a start. She felt tense and restless, and her mouth was dry, and she finally decided to get up and go to the kitchen for a glass of water. It was after midnight, but the light was still on in the dining room. Before she'd had time to realize why, Pardell had seen her.

"Sleepwalking?" he asked. "Or hungry."

She rubbed her eyes, blinking in the sudden glare. He was sitting at the dining room table surrounded by a huge stack of books and papers. He'd been there, doing research for a new article, three hours earlier when everyone else had gone to bed, but it hadn't occurred to her he'd still be there.

"Just thirsty," she said. "I couldn't sleep."

"You sure you're not hungry? I was just on my way to the kitchen for a peanut butter sandwich. Want to join me? I'll vouch for peanut butter as a sure-fire sedative. Knocks me out every time."

She said no again, but while she was drinking her

water, he was spreading peanut butter and the smell got to her. "I guess I'm changing my mind," she said.

"A human's prerogative," he said. "You catch that quick rewrite? Human's for woman's? I want my Brownie points for raised consciousness."

He slathered another piece of bread with peanut butter and poured a big glass of milk. "Here. Pull up a chair and dig in. You look famished." He paused, studying her face. "Hollow-eyed. Maybe not so much famished as—haunted. That's it, haunted. Restless spirits abroad tonight?"

It was strange because haunted was exactly the way she'd been feeling. Haunted by ghosts of the past as well as some new, dimly seen ones of the future. "I guess so," she said.

Afterwards she couldn't remember exactly how she started, but suddenly she was telling him about her plan, and how she'd taken the crucial step that afternoon at the Olivers', and how their reaction had been exactly what she'd hoped and planned for.

"In a way, it's like it was meant to be," she said. "I guess Sparrow is really a lot like their little girl who died, and they're both crazy about her. It was only Nan at first, but I think Richard is just as batty about her now. Or maybe even more so. Nan says he's that way. All or nothing at all; and once he makes up his mind about something, you'd better not get in his way."

Pardell was rubbing the bald spot on top of his head the way he always did when he was thinking hard. "And Oriole?" he asked. "Has she agreed to all this?"

"Not yet. But she will. On Monday, Richard and Nan are going to drive me to Ukiah to see her. I'll talk to her first, and then they'll come in. I'll tell her we'll just be going for a visit—nothing permanent or legal or anything—just a visit until she's out of jail and all. And then, if she gets out before the school year is up, we'll just write and say we want to stay until we've finished school. Then we'll come back for a while next summer. The Olivers promised me that we could. But when we tell her we want to go back to Connecticut in the fall, she'll let us go, I know. Oriole hasn't said no to me since I was about five years old. Besides, she'll be used to it by then. She'll see that it's the best for everyone. And eventually she'll probably let them adopt Sparrow. That's what they want to do."

"Is that what they said?"

"Sure. They'd do it in a minute if they could. Richard even wanted to offer to pay all of Oriole's lawyer's fees and a lot of other stuff, if she'd agree to an adoption right away. But I talked him out of that."

"Yeah," Pardell said. "That sounds like old Richard B., doesn't it."

Summer was puzzled. "Do you know him? Richard Oliver?"

"No. Not personally. But—" He paused. "—having read so much about him by a very acute and gifted journalist, I almost feel that I do."

"What do you mean?" Summer asked, but she really knew. She'd wondered, the night before when she discovered that she'd left the letter box on his desk, not only unlocked, but wide open. She couldn't imagine how she'd done such a thing. She'd never before, in all those years, left it unlocked even for a minute. But after the initial shock, she'd decided that he wouldn't have read the letters. He probably wouldn't even have wanted to. But she'd been wrong. Apparently he had.

"You did intend for me to read the letters, didn't you?" He looked concerned—worried.

"Oh, yes," she said quickly, and while she was saying it, she suddenly realized that it was true—one of those mistakes that at some deeper level wasn't a mistake at all.

"I've been wanting to talk to you about them," he said, "but I was waiting for you to bring it up. I thought maybe you needed a little more time to think about it."

She nodded. It would take some time. The fact that someone—that Pardell—had read all the letters to Grant was going to take a lot of thinking about. But at the moment her mind shied away, skittering fearfully around the edges of full realization. With everything else that was going on at the moment, it was just too much to deal with.

Pardell finally broke the silence. "So you don't think it would be a good idea for the Olivers to offer Oriole money?"

Almost with relief she brought her mind back to the immediate crisis. "No," she said firmly. "It would be the worst thing he could do. Oriole would freak out if she thought it was anything like—like selling us."

"But she could certainly use the money?"

189

"Well, yes. I guess so. But I don't think that would occur to her. Oriole is really strange about money. She never seems to worry about it." She smiled ruefully. "Hers, or anybody else's. It's something she just can't seem to keep her mind on."

"Hmm." Pardell was rubbing his head again. "As foibles go, I must say, that's a rather refreshing one."

"I suppose so." She'd never thought of it that way before.

"So you think she'll let you go if she's convinced it will be best for you. But don't you think it will be very hard for her later, when she comes back here—alone?"

Summer forced herself to continue to meet Pardell's eyes. "For a while, maybe. But Oriole never stays alone for very long. And she's never depressed for very long either." She smiled mockingly. "You know—bummed out? Oriole gets bummed out a lot, but she never stays that way. Even when things are really terrible, she's suddenly tripping out over some dumb little thing, like an animal or a nice day. I really don't think she'll miss us for very long. And besides—" Summer was talking fast, urgently, sounding, she knew, as if she were trying to convince herself as well as Pardell. "Besides, it will probably be easier for her to find some guy who will really stick around if she doesn't have two kids hanging around her neck." She stopped to stare at Pardell angrily. "What are you laughing about?"

"At the idea of you hanging around anybody's neck. Let me assure you, little friend, that I cannot imagine you as an albatross—as a weight around any-

190

one's neck, that is. And I mean that as a compliment. As a superlative compliment, in fact."

Her eyes wavered, then, and fell. She'd always found it easier to face up to criticism and disapproval than to a compliment.

"However," Pardell went on, "it seems to me that, as usual, your assessment of the situation is fairly accurate, at least as far as Oriole is concerned. But how about Sparrow? Do you really think that life as a substitute Debbie would be the best thing for Sparrow?"

"I know. I've thought about it a lot. Particularly lately. When we were out there, I almost decided it wouldn't. It's just that staying here with Oriole is going to be about the worst possible thing for her. I'm sure of that. I'm going to go away to college soon, and she'll be here alone with Oriole and—the thing is, they're so much alike. For people like Sparrow and Oriole, it's so much a matter of chance. You know. It's fate, or the times, or the people they meet. They're just like mirrors, reflecting back whatever they see."

"And you think Sparrow will be happy reflecting back the Olivers."

She shrugged. "Pretty much. The thing is, there's a lot that she just won't see."

"Like?"

"Like?" She grinned. "Like smug—and stuffed shirt—and the way they're so sure they're right about everything."

"I see. And that brings us to another question. How about Summer—who does see? How about a sixteen-year-old who sees with remarkable clarity? Where is she going to fit into this arrangement?"

Her smile admitted that he'd hit on a tender spot. "Who knows?" she said.

"What I gathered from the letters is that their interest in you is a bit different."

"I know. With me it's more like, 'the best little parlor maid they've ever been able to lay their hands on.' "

"Knock it off, kid," Pardell said. "You know it's more than that. I gather that they are very impressed and admire you very much. It's just that you didn't happen to be a seven-year-old who resembled their lost daughter. But I agree that it looks like your situation at the Olivers' is going to be rather ambiguous. Particularly if Sparrow is going to be family, and perhaps you aren't."

She shrugged again, grinning. "So what? Life is hard. And besides, I'll get the same fringe benefits. Like no more food stamps, for instance."

But Pardell didn't smile back. "Okay," he said, making it sound like "okay, if you want to be that way." "But there's another consideration. What about you—and Oriole. What about needing to know about Oriole, when she's three thousand miles away. You can't run three thousand miles."

Anger flared immediately. He had no right. No right to read her letters and then talk about something so private. So private that ever since it had begun when she first started school, she'd never mentioned it to anyone—except Grant, of course. Clenching her teeth she turned her head away.

192

He waited, and it wasn't until she breathed deeply and started to turn back, that he said, "I'm sorry, Summer. But it's something you should think about."

"I have. And it's all right. It's all over. Ever since the night of the raid. I knew it the next day. It's like, well, it started when I first had to be away from her. I was always afraid she'd be dead or gone when I came back, and back then that was like the end of the world. And even after I knew it wouldn't be, I couldn't stop feeling, not in my mind but somewhere else, that it would. But when I woke up after that night, I knew that, in a way, it had happened, and it hadn't been the end of the world. And I wasn't ever going to have to run home again."

"Okay. Good. I believe you. But in a way running is what you're planning to do. A different kind of running. A hard-headed, well-thought-out kind, this time. But it is running. And the thing is—you don't need to. You don't need Connecticut. Sparrow —maybe. I'm inclined to agree with you about that. But not you, Summer. Oh, it won't be fatal if you go. Unpleasant at times and probably fairly infuriating, but you'll come out all right. But the thing is, you would anyway. I'm as convinced of that as I am that the sun's going to be coming up"—he glanced toward the window—"before very long. You'll be a great success in Connecticut, just as you would be right here in Alvarro Bay, in spite of all the people who've enjoyed being sure that you wouldn't, all these years. And in spite of Oriole, too."

She was angry again. He was just trying to confuse her. It was none of his business, and she resented it. She couldn't say so with words, but there was a better way. She stood up and started to leave.

"Come back here," he said, and to her surprise, she did. When she was staring at him, frowning and clenching her jaw, he said. "And one more thing. If you run off to Connecticut to live by scheming and conniving, which, by the way, you're very good at, you'll be throwing away one of your greatest assets. Did you realize that? Granted you've got assets to spare—I mean, smart, capable, self-disciplined, but the one that's really unique is the way you feel about Sparrow—and Oriole. Yes, and Oriole—underneath all the disillusionment and frustration. It looks to me as if you're planning to trade in a really unique talent for love and loyalty on a bowl of security pottage, and a not very—"

She didn't hear the rest because she left the room and shut the door firmly behind her. She'd have slammed it if it hadn't been for Sparrow.

It was beginning to get light when she got up and turned on the gooseneck lamp over Pardell's desk. Tearing a page off one of his long yellow tablets she began to write.

> *Dear Grant,*
>
> *I've been thinking—most of the night, actually. And I've finally decided that I don't really want to go to Connecticut after all. So I'll just tell Oriole that it's too hard for me to take care of Sparrow all by myself, and the Olivers have made this offer to take*

care of her for a while. I know Oriole will agree to that, and then there'll be lots of time to deal with what happens next. Sparrow won't want to go without me, but I can talk her into it. She won't miss me for long and it will be easier for her to be an Oliver without me there to complicate things.

But that's not the reason I'm not going. The real reason is that I don't want to. I never did, really. I'll go away soon enough, but not now and not to Connecticut. And when I do go, it will be to someplace I choose for myself, and where I can go on making my own choices.

That's all for now because I'm finally getting sleepy.

Love,
Summer

She put the letter on top of all the others, and then closed and locked the box and climbed into the hide-a-bed, shoving Sparrow over to her own side. A minute later she got up again, unlocked the box and took the letter out. Clearing off a spot amid the Pardellian shambles, she spread out the yellow sheet, right in front of his chair, where he'd have to see it. Halfway back in bed, she stopped again. Back at the desk she grabbed a pen and drew a line through the word "Grant." Then she drew several more lines until it was entirely crossed out. She thought for a moment, and then, in place of the crossed-out name, she wrote—"Alan."